SECRETS UNDER THE COVERS
(Silverberry Seduction Seasoned Romance Series, Book One)

By Brenda Margriet

COPYRIGHT PAGE

SECRETS UNDER THE COVERS
(Silverberry Seduction Seasoned Romance Series, Book One)

Originally released in A SEASON FOR LOVE Anthology
March 1, 2022

This edition published August 2022
Copyright © 2022 Brenda Margriet Clotildes
E-book: 978-1-7773513-8-0
Print: 978-1-7773513-7-3

Cover Art by K. B. Barrett Designs

Excerpt from
LOVING BETWEEN THE LINES
(Silverberry Seduction Seasoned Romance Series,
Book Two)

First edition published July 2022
Copyright © 2022 Brenda Margriet Clotildes
Digital ISBN 978-1-7773513-6-6
Print ISBN 978-1-7773513-5-9

Reaching behind her back in that double-jointed way women had, Helen fiddled with something then rolled her shoulders. The straps slipped down her arms and the dress swept over her hips to the floor.

Nathan's breath caught.

She waved her hand in his direction. "Your turn." She began tossing the many pillows mounded at the head of the bed onto the floor with abandon.

The satiny white panties and bra she wore offset her tanned legs, shoulders, and arms. But what stunned him into immobility was—

"Tattoos? I didn't know you had tattoos!"

She threw him a saucy look as she folded the duvet neatly back to the foot of the mattress. "I work at a tattoo parlor, Nathan. Is it so surprising?"

Helen had been a high school art teacher for thirty years but had retired when Aaron got sick. A couple of years ago she had taken a part-time job at a tattoo parlor "for something to do."

"How many do you have?" As if drawn by a magnet, he drifted toward her. Above the edge of her panties, on her right hip, was a red rose on a thin green stem, about an inch long all together.

"Two." She straightened from the bed and faced him. Loosening the strap of her bra by slipping it down her bicep, she folded the cup back far enough to reveal a heart. "For my mom," she said.

He knew she'd lost her mother to breast cancer well before she'd married Aaron, and her father to a heart attack about fifteen years ago. While she talked freely about her dad, she rarely mentioned her mother. It made the fact she'd had a permanent reminder inked onto her skin especially poignant.

"You must miss her." His parents were both hale and hearty, and he gave silent thanks.

"She's been gone a long time." Before he could wonder about the emotions hidden behind that cool acceptance, she cocked a hand on her hip and waggled her finger at him. "Why are you still dressed?"

To everyone who was there the first time I tried a Red Shoe Martini, and to Girls' Nights past, present, and future. Laughing until we cry, eating too much, drinking more than we should...ah, good times.

Chapter One

You've been here before. *There's nothing to worry about.*

Helen Mansfield shifted restlessly, the paper sheet on the examination table rustling under her. Maybe she should have sat on the chair in the corner. This was a routine meeting to discuss the results—the sure-to-be absolutely, totally normal, nothing to worry about results—of the ultrasound she'd had done as a follow up to her annual mammogram.

To distract herself, she tried to count the number of cotton balls in the glass jar with the tin lid on the counter in front of her. It sat next to a similar jar of wooden tongue depressors. Both seemed oddly out of place next to the sleek, black flat-screen monitor attached to the wall by a swinging arm. Did doctors still use wooden tongue depressors? Wasn't there something a little more...sophisticated by now?

The door opened without warning, and Dr. Shelagh Chesley strode in. She'd been Helen's family doctor for more than three decades and, while they didn't socialize, Helen considered her a friend, one who had been with her through the birth of her daughter, years of sore throats and upset stomachs, a bout with pneumonia, the onset of menopause.

And the death of Helen's husband from pancreatic cancer three years ago.

"Hello, Shelagh." She licked her lips, mouth dry with nerves, despite her internal pep talk.

"Helen." Dr. Chesley leaned against the counter and crossed her arms, her navy-blue blazer tightening across her shoulders. Her hair was unapologetically steel grey, cut in a short bob, and her makeup understated. "I'm going to come right out and say it— the ultrasound confirmed a mass in your right breast. We need to biopsy, so we know exactly what we're dealing with."

"Are you sure?" Helen winced. "Of course you're sure. It's just, I've had abnormal mammograms before. We've even gone as far as an ultrasound. There's never been a need for a biopsy."

"You know you have dense breast tissue. That often means additional scans to rule out areas of concern. And you're right, we've never had to go further than an ultrasound. Until now. Given your family history, we can't discount what we're seeing this time."

Helen's mother had died from breast cancer at forty-three, when Helen was only twenty. Now fifty-five, she'd outlived her mother by a dozen years, but that turbulent time still had the power to make her stomach roil. When her mother's younger sister had required a double mastectomy and passed away from the same disease a few years later, Helen had met with Shelagh to discuss preventative measures.

And here they were.

Helen couldn't say the word, fearful of conjuring it into reality. But she needed to know. "What are your instincts telling you?"

Dr. Chesley pressed her lips together. "I won't speculate, Helen. Given the characteristics of what we've seen in the mammogram and ultrasound, I want to do a surgical biopsy and remove the mass. I've arranged for you to go in a week from tomorrow. It's an outpatient procedure done with local anesthetic and a mild sedative, so you'll need someone to drive you home."

It was all going too fast. Helen held up her hand. "Hold on. Isn't there something else we can do before we go full bore with *surgery*?"

"No." Dr. Chesley regarded Helen with a compassion that made her even more queasy. It was exactly the expression she'd expect to see on the face of a doctor giving bad news. "It's a small lump, and I am confident we can remove it entirely during the biopsy. Next steps will be determined once we know exactly what we're dealing with."

Helen floated untethered from her feet, and made her way out of the doctor's office, into the elevator, and out the exterior doors to where her car was parked. She slid into the driver's seat, the air of the interior stifling and stale. July had been unusually hot for northern British Columbia, and there was no end in sight for the soaring temperatures.

Despite the heat, Helen shivered. A chunk of ice sat low in her belly, the chill of fear creeping through her nerves and veins. She cupped her hand over her right breast and pressed. She couldn't feel anything—wasn't even sure exactly where the lump was. She pictured it, an oozing, pernicious mass radiating its evil tendrils deep into her body.

Then she pictured smashing it with a hammer, stomping it under her foot, crushing it with a rock so big she had to clutch it with both hands.

Feeling slightly steadier, she started the engine and pulled out of the parking lot.

Something was wrong with Helen.

Nathan Spieth chatted with Stephanie Collins

while keeping an eye on Helen. She flitted about, the skirt of her lightweight summer dress fluttering above her knees, the Red Shoe Martini she held sloshing but never spilling from its wide-mouthed glass, making sure everyone had a drink and was helping themselves to snacks. He didn't think any of the other members of the Silverberry Book Club—meeting this Tuesday evening in Helen's back yard—had noticed anything. But he'd long been attuned to even the slightest changes in her mood.

Something was definitely not right in her world.

"All right, everyone!" She called the group to attention by tapping lightly on her martini glass with her fingernail. "Let's gather round and start the discussion."

Nathan offered Stephanie a seat on the deep cushion of the outdoor sofa. This was her first book club meeting, and she seemed rather shy and bewildered. She had come with Terrance Renfrew and his husband Bennett, but the couple had become involved in a conversation with Penta Potter, another member of the Silverberries, and left Stephanie standing awkwardly alone. Nathan had stepped into his unofficial role as secondary host and set himself to putting the new arrival at ease.

Once everyone was settled, Helen launched the analysis of last month's assigned reading. Nathan watched her closely, contributing when needed to keep the conversation going, but otherwise letting the six or so other members carry the ball. The book club had been active for a little over two years, but he'd sensed for a couple of months now that interest was waning. Part of that might have something to do with the wonderful weather they'd been having. Who wanted to sit around discussing "good" books when they could be out on a boat or at a cabin or generally enjoying the heat wave? Meeting on Helen's deck had been a compromise, yet even so several regulars had made their excuses and not attended.

An hour later, the discussion broke up. Nathan began collecting the party's detritus while Helen escorted the rest of the Silverberries to the front yard. He lived right next door—had for twenty years—and it was habit for him and Helen to help the other with clean up when it was their turn to host. Given Helen's demeanour this evening, he had an additional motive for sticking around.

She returned from the front yard and climbed the wooden steps to the deck. Normally brimming over with energy and verve, she moved at a slower pace tonight and the creases around her mouth were deeper than usual.

As he placed dirty glasses of all shapes and sizes on a serving tray, he said casually, "Everything all right?"

"Of course." Her reply came so quickly he knew it was a reflex, not necessarily the truth.

He straightened and pinned her with a glance. "Helen. I've known you a long time. There's something on your mind."

She averted her gaze and began stacking serving dishes with abrupt, jerky movements. "It's nothing important."

Nathan studied her. Three years ago, when her husband Aaron had died, she'd stopped colouring her hair and had chopped the long silvery locks into a skull-hugging cut that accentuated her cheekbones and amazing green eyes. A muscle in her jaw flexed repeatedly and, well acquainted with her innate stubbornness, he decided to leave the subject be. For now.

They worked in silence, moving around each other with the ease and efficiency of years of practice. He reflected on how they'd come to this stage in their relationship. When they'd met, they'd both been married. Nathan's three sons and Helen's only daughter had been in elementary school. Now they were both widowed. He had three grandchildren, she one granddaughter.

He'd found Helen attractive from their first meeting, in a general, appreciative way. As he'd grown more and more dissatisfied with his own marriage, though, he'd done his best to squash any show of interest. The difficulties Wanda and he were going through were complicated enough without adding in lust for their next-door neighbour—especially since that neighbour was very happily married and had no idea what he was feeling. Then, just when he'd raised the courage to discuss divorce with Wanda, she'd been diagnosed with breast cancer, and, well, he'd stayed.

Now she had been gone five years, and his sharp, stabbing guilt had faded. What still stood out keen and clear were the months leading up to her final day. It was one more thing he and Helen had in common. Though his love for Wanda had faded well before her diagnosis—unlike Helen's feelings for Aaron—watching someone you'd built a life and family with die of cancer was not an experience he ever wanted to live through again, and he was sure Helen felt the same way.

A clattering smash jolted him from his thoughts. Helen stood at the sink, the chip and dip bowls, vegetable platter, and sundry other dishes in a heap inside it. She gripped the edge of the counter and rocked back and forth, her head bowed.

"Helen?" Alarmed, he stepped forward, tossing aside the dish rag he'd been using to wipe the kitchen island and resting his hand on her forearm. "Now you've got to tell me. What's going on?"

She looked up, her eyes wide and wild, a pulse beating rapidly in her throat.

"Do you want to have sex?" she said.

Chapter Two

Nathan's face went blank, and a flush raced up Helen's neck. *What have I done?*

He blinked. "Do I *what*?"

She swallowed. "I haven't had sex since Aaron died. I think it's time." It was the first excuse that came to mind. She couldn't tell Nathan her secret—that she needed to wring every last ounce of enjoyment out of life while she could. That would put unfair pressure on him, and unlike her mother, Helen refused to resort to emotional blackmail.

Nathan lost his stunned expression, and his intense blue eyes focused on hers. "I thought that was what you said. But I wanted to make sure."

His light grip on her forearm strengthened. She wondered if he could feel the frantic pulse beating in her wrist. She lifted her chin. "So? Do you?"

He tilted his head and his palm swept up to her shoulder and down again. Goosebumps rippled in the wake of his caress. The urge to celebrate every moment of life, the same urge that had initiated her invitation, heated into something deeper. It had been a long time since she'd felt the power of her sexuality, and it flooded her senses like rain on dry land.

"Why now?" Nathan stepped closer. The warmth of his body enveloped her, unimpeded by his short-sleeved shirt and dress shorts. "Does it have something to do with what's been bothering you tonight?"

"No," she lied. "It's just...time. And I thought...sometimes you seem..." She stuttered to a stop. What if she was wrong? What if Nathan *hadn't* been giving her admiring glances, sending off faint signals of attraction? She couldn't pinpoint when she'd started to notice those tiny hints a man gives a woman, but it had been a while now.

Hadn't it?

She stepped backward, pulling her arm from his gentle clasp. "Never mind. Forget I said anything."

He paced forward and she took another involuntary step back, coming up against the floor-to-ceiling cabinets that lined one wall of her kitchen. He followed again, standing so close he left barely a breath of air between them.

She was suddenly, overwhelmingly aware of every inch of her bare skin. And his.

"Helen."

His voice was whisper soft but held a note of command she couldn't ignore. She lifted her gaze from her contemplation of the stitching on his breast pocket.

"I very much want to have sex with you," he said. "I have for a long time. But I didn't think you felt the same way about me."

She hadn't thought so, either. Nathan had been a friend for so long she'd stopped *seeing* him. They were more than neighbours. Watching him lose Wanda, having him at her side during Aaron's illness, had forged a different, undefinable relationship between them. But she certainly hadn't regarded him *sexually*.

Yet, since Dr. Chesley's unsettling news this afternoon, she'd been under a growing compulsion to prove she was still alive, that she still had a place in this world. Sex—even sex after menopause—was an affirmation of life, and the more she'd thought about it, the more she'd thought about Nathan. Watching him this evening had made her edgy and uncomfortable in a way she hadn't been since her twenties.

He was waiting for her reply, with the patient look she was accustomed to seeing back on his face. Gathering her courage, she placed one palm flat against his chest. "I do feel that way."

Nathan braced his hands flat on the cupboards on either side of her head. The muscles under her palm bunched and shifted and she placed her other hand beside the first to savour the sensation even more. Slowly, oh, so slowly, he leaned in and pressed his lips to hers, holding his body away so their mouths and her hands were their only points of contact.

If they'd ever kissed before in their long friendship, Helen couldn't remember when. There had been casual hugs and consoling embraces, but had their lips ever touched? His were smooth and cool, motionless, undemanding, and she felt a pang of disappointment. Where was the zing, the sizzle, the passion she so wanted and needed?

Downcast, her shoulders relaxed. As if he'd been waiting for such a signal of surrender, Nathan's kiss changed.

He increased the pressure, and his tongue traced the seam of her closed lips. Instinctively she opened her mouth, and he delved inside with small, tantalizing touches. He tasted faintly of the beer he'd had earlier.

He gave a small grunt and raised his head, an amused gleam in his eyes. "You're pulling hairs."

Her hands had fisted in his shirt. She snatched them away. "Sorry."

"Don't be. I'll take that as a good sign." He returned to her mouth, nipping and sucking and licking and suddenly all the sizzle she'd wanted was right *there*, burning through her nerve endings, sparking between her legs, swelling her breasts.

She wound her arms around his neck and arched her back. His thigh wedged between hers and she wriggled against him, hooking one bare leg around his calf, the dusting of wiry hairs erotic against her smoother skin.

His hands were still planted on the cupboard doors. "Touch me," she muttered against his mouth. "I need you to touch me."

He gripped her hips and pulled her closer. She purred with approval, her fingers dancing on the nape of his neck, and then cupped his skull and swept her palm to the crown of his head. He kept his hair short and the change from bristles to smoothness came as a tiny shock. She'd known he was balding, of course, but feeling the difference was a different sort of knowing.

She liked the sleekness of his scalp.

The slide and rustle of fabric tickled her thighs as he bunched her dress at her waist. With a practiced movement he swept his hands under the skirt and gripped her ass, lifting her onto her toes. Her thin satin panties were no barrier to the heat emanating from his palms. With joy she felt a rush of dampness between her legs and rubbed herself against his thigh. He stepped in, squashing her delightfully between his body and the wood behind her.

Speaking of wood. With dazed bawdiness, she revelled in the heated length of his erection hard against her belly. Was there anything more satisfying for a woman than this incontrovertible proof of a man's desire? The power made her dizzy.

All the while, their mouths had been searching, exploring, tasting. She dragged her lips far enough away to speak. "Bedroom?"

"God, yes."

In a haze of sexual longing and rampant desire, Nathan followed Helen down the hall and up the stairs, their hands entwined. He didn't want to lose contact, afraid severing their link would cause her to change her mind.

She tugged him into the large master bedroom overlooking the front yard. When Aaron had been ill, Nathan had spent many afternoons in this room keeping his friend company in order to give Helen much-needed respite. But since his death, there'd been no reason for Nathan to come to the second floor.

"You painted." The dark burgundy walls had been replaced with a pale lemon tint. The furniture was the same heavy wood, but instead of the forest green bedding and striped curtains he'd expected, the duvet cover was a natural-looking linen with pale blue accents and the window hidden by light sheers. It was altogether a brighter, more feminine space, and it suited Helen perfectly.

"Can we discuss decor later?" Her grin took any possible sting from her words. Reaching behind her back in that double-jointed way women had, she fiddled with something then rolled her shoulders. The straps slipped down her arms and the dress swept over her hips to the floor.

His cock hardened further as his breath caught.

She waved her hand in his direction. "Your turn." She began tossing the many pillows mounded at the head of the bed onto the floor with abandon.

The satiny white panties and bra she wore offset her tanned legs, shoulders, and arms. But what stunned him into immobility was—

"Tattoos? I didn't know you had tattoos!"

She threw him a saucy look as she folded the duvet neatly back to the foot of the mattress. "I work at a tattoo parlor, Nathan. Is it so surprising?"

Helen had been a high school art teacher for thirty years but had retired when Aaron got sick. A couple of years ago she had taken a part-time job as a receptionist at a tattoo parlor "for something to do."

"How many do you have?" As if drawn by a magnet, he drifted toward her. Above the edge of her panties, on her right hip, was a red rose on a thin green stem, about an inch long all together.

"Two." She straightened from the bed and faced him. Loosening the strap of her bra by slipping it down her bicep, she folded the cup back far enough to reveal a heart. "For my mom," she said.

He knew she'd lost her mother to breast cancer well before she'd married Aaron, and her father to a heart attack about fifteen years ago. While she talked freely about her dad, she rarely mentioned her mother. It made the fact she'd had a permanent reminder inked onto her skin especially poignant.

"You must miss her." His parents were both hale and hearty, and he gave silent thanks.

"She's been gone a long time." Before he could wonder about the emotions hidden behind that cool acceptance, she cocked a hand on her hip and waggled her eyebrows at him. "Why are you still dressed?"

Chapter Three

Nathan pulled his shirt over his head, feeling oddly self-conscious. It wasn't as if Helen had never seen his naked torso before. Their families had spent time together at lakes and pools and even a joint vacation in Mexico. But that had been years ago, and his male pattern baldness bothered him less than the fact his stomach was not as flat as it used to be and the hairs on his chest were grey and wiry.

Helen strode forward without a shade of hesitancy or awkwardness. She trailed a fingertip from the hollow at the base of his throat, down his breastbone, past his bellybutton and to the waistband of his shorts. The fit was loose and his erection obvious. He hissed as that teasing finger traced his length, tapping the tip and making him jerk.

Her smile was feline, crafty. "Let me help." She slipped the button through its hole and reached for the zipper tab. He sucked in a breath and her grin grew. "Don't worry, I'll be careful."

She inched the fastener down and, when she had room to maneuver, slid her hand inside his jockeys and clasped him firmly.

"Oh, god." Nathan's eyes closed and he gripped

her hips for support.

"You feel so good. Hot. Heavy." Her fingers moved up and down, playing, discovering. "I've missed this. I've missed touching a man, having a man touch me."

Helen's reminder of her husband could have troubled Nathan, but it didn't. Given her recent words and actions, as well as the flush on her neck and the gleam in her eyes, it appeared she enjoyed sex. If she'd learned that with Aaron, Nathan had no complaints. He'd gladly be the beneficiary of her enthusiasm now.

He groaned in dismay when she released him to shimmy his clothing over his hips. She bent forward to help him step out and he swept his hands along the bumps in her spine, admiring the curve and sway of her buttocks, the dip at her lower back.

She straightened and her breath on his thigh as she lifted her head just about sent him over the edge. It had been a long time since he'd had sex, too. He'd had two short-lived relationships after Wanda died, both stunted by his focus on work and unwillingness to define his commitment.

As well as his continued attraction to Helen, even though her attention had been on supporting then mourning Aaron.

Now naked, he wrapped his arms around her torso and pulled her tight. Her softness and heat moulded against him, her hands on his back, her hips pressed against his groin. Their lips fused, tongues tangled, and the flare of his desire rose higher and higher. He flicked open the rear fastening of her bra and without releasing her mouth, slipped it from her body. Her nipples were hard points against his chest, and he cupped her plush breasts with reverence.

"I've waited—" He stopped, a faint sense of self-preservation warning him not to admit how long he'd wanted to touch her like this. Confessing he'd desired her years before either of their spouses had passed away might not go over well.

"What?" She spoke absently, her attention on his neck, her nibbling bites zinging sparks along his nerve endings.

"Let's lay down."

Appearing not to notice his non sequitur, she slipped off her panties and climbed on the bed, laying her head against the single pillow she'd left there. The pulse pounding in his groin thickened as he surveyed her, lush and open. "You're beautiful." He sat beside her, one foot on the floor, one knee drawn up on the mattress.

"You don't have to say things like that." She swept her hand up and down her naked body. "I'm going to have sex with you no matter what."

He heard a shyness behind her teasing tone and met her gaze seriously. "You...are...beautiful," he repeated, spacing his words deliberately, and following up his declaration with strokes and caresses with his hands and mouth.

She responded fiercely and freely, writhing under his ministrations. Her thighs trembled, her hands gripped his skull, and with a shocking suddenness her first orgasm rippled through her.

Several minutes later she was damp and panting, moaning she could take no more, and he felt a masculine pride that he'd been able to bring her to such limp satiation. Settling between her thighs, his cock nestled at her centre, he braced his elbows on either side of her head and stared down at her flushed face.

"Are you sure about this?" It might kill him, but if she'd changed her mind, he could still stop. What came next would change their relationship forever. A tiny yet rational part of his brain was still wondering what had caused her to issue her proposition—but a lusty and larger part didn't care why. Not at all.

"More than sure." Her fingers dug into his hips, and she wriggled until he nudged her entrance.

His relief at her assurance was all encompassing, yet he gritted his teeth, leashing his desire. *One more thing.* "What about a condom?"

She froze. "Do we need one? I haven't been with anyone since Aaron. And I'm past menopause." Her eyes widened. "Nathan Spieth! What have you been up to?"

"Nothing! I haven't been with anyone for two years. You know that."

"Just because you haven't introduced me to anyone doesn't mean you haven't been sneaking around."

She seemed rather pleased at the idea he might have slept with other women. What did that mean? Then she slid one hand between them and gripped his cock, rubbing it against her wetness, and he could barely remember his own name, let alone worry about what she believed of his escapades.

"I want you inside me," she whispered, lifting her hips.

He slid home, shuddering, and buried his face in the curve of her neck.

Helen wrapped her arms and legs around Nathan, feeling the muscles in his back and thighs flexing and rippling as he thrust inside her.

She'd forgotten how wonderful the sensation of fullness was, how intimate and joyful the connection with another human being could be. Nathan had coaxed liquid, rolling orgasms out of her with his fingers and tongue, and she was more than happy to let him take his own satisfaction from her body now. Tenderness swept through her, and she whispered encouragement, urging him on, until with one last deep plunge he stiffened and groaned, and then slowly collapsed on top of her.

Tears welled and she blinked them away, shocked at the depth of her emotions. Gratitude for the gift they had shared filled her. No matter what happened with the biopsy, she'd had this night with a man she loved. Maybe not as she'd loved Aaron, but one she loved as a friend, a confidante. She trusted Nathan implicitly, was incredibly thankful for his acceptance of her invitation. She knew she couldn't impose on him like this again. It had been an impulse, a life-affirming quest, not something to be repeated.

He shifted and her arms tightened. Heeding her wordless request, he relaxed again, his weight warm and welcome like a comforting blanket. His head rested on the pillow next to hers, his face turned toward her, his breathing slowing and gentling, puffing in her ear with a ticklish touch.

When her embrace loosened a few minutes later, Nathan rolled onto his side, bending one elbow to support his head. She could feel his gaze but didn't meet his eyes.

"Thank you," she said, keeping her tone light. "I think I needed that."

"You're welcome."

Forestalling anything else he might have been planning to say, she asked, "What time is it?"

Nathan looked over his shoulder to the nightstand where her alarm clock stood. "Two minutes after ten."

"You'll be wanting to get home, I guess."

"Helen..."

Unexpectedly petrified at what he might say next, she scrambled to the edge of the bed and stood. "This isn't going to make things awkward between us, is it?"

He rolled off the opposite side of the mattress and they faced each other across the queen-sized expanse. "Maybe we should have thought of that before."

Helen wished she had a robe handy to wrap herself in. Naked before Nathan in the heat of sex was one thing. Naked in the cooling afterglow was just...weird.

"I'm sorry. I wasn't thinking very clearly when I asked you."

"Don't apologize." Nathan's eyes narrowed. "You didn't exactly force me. I could have said no."

She opened her mouth to ask why he hadn't done that exact thing, and then closed it with a snap. On second thought, she didn't want to know why her friend of twenty years had decided to have sex with her. Her own reasons were muddied and selfish and tied up in fear. She didn't want to hear he had the same issues.

The silence between them grew fraught and edgy. Helen made herself meet Nathan's direct gaze. His pale blue eyes regarded her calmly, and some of her nervousness dissipated. "It's too late to change our minds now. We'll have to deal with it." Ignoring her nudity, she walked around the foot of the bed and held out her hand. "Friends still?"

He studied her face a moment longer, and then gave one sharp jerk of his chin in a brisk nod. "Friends." He clasped her hand, shook it, and released her.

Though she knew this night didn't mean anything, that it had been the impulse of the moment for both of them, she felt a stab of regret. He hadn't had to agree quite so quickly, had he? Annoyed with herself, she stepped back. "Do you want to clean up before you go?"

"I'll use the hall bathroom." He gathered his shorts and shirt from the floor. "Goodnight, Helen."

"Goodnight."

He strode out of the bedroom. She released a sigh of relief when his naked ass disappeared. Time apart was what they needed to get back on an even keel, to rebuild the cozy comfortableness of their friendship.

Yet as she headed to the en suite to take a shower, an unexpected weight of loneliness rested on her shoulders.

Chapter Four

"Gramma!" Nora raced through the front door with her usual abandon and flung her arms around Helen's knees.

"Hey, sweet pea, how are you?" Helen always looked forward to Wednesdays, the day she babysat her four-year-old granddaughter. Today she was more than pleased to have such a delightful distraction from the events of the day and night before.

The worrisome need for a biopsy.

The head-banging sex with Nathan.

"Can we go to the water park today?" Nora peered up, short blonde pigtails dangling, blue eyes bright with innocent manipulation. "Pretty please with sugar on top?"

Helen laughed and booped her snubbed nose. "I don't see why not. It's going to be another scorcher."

"Hi, Mom." Megan followed her daughter much more sedately. She placed Nora's pink sequined backpack on the floor. "She's been talking about the water park for ages, so I brought her swimsuit in case you were up for it."

Helen stifled the pinch of resentment at the implication she was too old to take her granddaughter to the park. Megan didn't mean it that way. She hoped. "It's a great idea. We'll have fun." She turned her attention back to Nora. "I made the batter for our pancakes. Why don't you go give it a stir while I talk to your mom for a minute?" They always had breakfast together on these days, and pancakes were Nora's favourite.

"Yum!" Nora ran to the kitchen and seconds later Helen heard the scrape of the snooping stool as Nora positioned it to reach the counter.

"What's going on?" Not for the first time, Helen wished Megan weren't *quite* so observant. Intuitiveness was an excellent trait for Dr. Megan Willson but could be rather irritating in a daughter whose diaper she'd changed and tears she'd dried.

"Nothing important." Helen smiled, hiding her discomfort at her white lie. "But I won't be able to take Nora next week."

"That shouldn't be a problem if I remember Nicholas's schedule correctly." Megan's husband was a dentist who worked twelve-hour days in a pattern that seemed confusingly random to Helen. She thought she'd gotten away without providing further details, until Megan narrowed her eyes. "So...why can't you take her?"

Other people might be thrilled to have a doctor in the family, especially after they'd been given bad news about their health. Helen knew she wasn't *other people*. She needed to protect her secret as long as possible.

When her mother had been diagnosed, she'd expected a nineteen-year-old Helen to abandon her life, come rushing home from university. Out from under her parent's domineering thumb for the first time and attending school on a scholarship that couldn't be deferred, Helen had taken a stand for her independence and refused. Frequent visits hadn't been enough to placate her mother, and the rift had only widened through the months of her illness. Helen would never lay such a guilt trip on Megan.

If the biopsy were clear, there'd be no need to tell her anything. If it weren't—well, she'd deal with it then. Megan was aware of the family history of breast cancer, and this would affect her personally. Better to let sleeping dogs lie until absolutely necessary.

"They need me at Golden Dragon," Helen said. "The receptionist that does Monday to Wednesday is away." Helen's regular shifts at the tattoo parlor were Thursday and Friday. She didn't like lying to Megan, but she'd had to prepare an excuse, and this had seemed the simplest.

"You've never had to cover before." Megan's scrutiny made her look every inch Dr. Willson.

Helen felt exposed, as if the tumour were a glowing beacon flashing its cruel message for all to see. "Of course I have. It just hasn't interfered with looking after Nora." Helen tried to sound nonchalant but was sure she failed miserably.

"So that means you can't take her at all, then? You're working all five days?"

Helen hesitated. She hadn't thought past the day of the biopsy, and Megan's question reminded her she'd have to arrange to take Thursday and Friday off, as per Dr. Chesley's instructions for recuperation after the surgery. "No, I can't. I'm sorry."

"Nora will be disappointed."

"I'll make it up to her."

Megan's piercing stare relaxed, and she lifted a corner of her mouth in a small smile. "Ice cream works."

Helen grinned back, relieved Megan appeared to have accepted her explanation. "Like mother, like daughter."

"I should get to the office." Megan hesitated in the doorway, the picture of professionalism in a sleeveless white tank and a deep pink pencil skirt with coordinating pumps. Her features were a more delicate version of Aaron's, and she had his dark hair and brown eyes. Helen couldn't help a rush of pride for her successful, intelligent, beautiful daughter.

"Mom?" Megan tilted her head thoughtfully. "You'd tell me if there was something I needed to know, right?"

"Of course." That definitely wasn't a lie. There was nothing to tell Megan yet. But when—*if*—there was, Helen would be sure to couch the news as positively as possible, to avoid alarming Megan or giving her the impression Helen needed help. Her daughter had her own life to live, and Helen refused to lay any extra burdens on her. She would handle this on her own, as she always had.

"Okay." Megan tapped her short nails on the door frame in a restless tattoo. "Love you."

They weren't the type of family that said such things out loud that often. The tears that seemed to come so easily since yesterday welled again, and she willed them away. "Love you, too."

A rapid knocking dragged Nathan's attention from the spreadsheet on the computer monitor in front of him. Head still swirling with figures, he blinked at the woman standing in his office doorway. "Hey."

"Got a minute?" Melanie Devane was the Regional Sales Manager for Nechako Industrial Supply, where Nathan had worked most of his adult life. She was also his direct supervisor.

"Of course. What can I do for you?" He leaned back in his seat and waved her in.

She dropped into one of the visitor chairs and crossed her legs. "It's more what I can do for you." Her eyes gleamed with bright intelligence. As a woman in what was predominately a man's world—the company provided tools and equipment for the forestry and mining sectors—she was fiercely determined and took no shit from anyone.

"I know you wanted my job," she said. "I mean, before I got it. When it was available five years ago."

"Yes, I did." It wasn't a secret, but he was a little blindsided by Melanie's blunt reference. Not that she was ever anything *but* blunt. Her forthrightness was one of the many things he liked and respected about her, and all those things together had tempered his severe disappointment at not being awarded the position.

Nathan had joined Nechako Industrial Supply more than twenty-five years ago, starting as lowly counter staff before rising rapidly to local sales. He'd built up his client list with slow and steady improvements, and becoming regional manager, which involved overseeing all account executives in northern British Columbia, was the next logical step in his career. He *had* wanted the promotion, and rather badly.

But life was all about timing. When the position had become available, Wanda had been fighting cancer for a couple of years, and they'd just learned it had spread to her lungs. While he could have sought forgetfulness in work, he had barely enough energy to keep up with his familiar, day-to-day duties, let alone take on a whole new level of responsibility. The opportunity passed and he'd hidden the burning regret as best he could.

Melanie tilted her head, regarding him intently, reminding him of a sparrow. Short and thin, with brown hair sprinkled with grey, the bird-like impression was enhanced by the drab colours she preferred to wear. "Your boys live on Vancouver Island, right?"

Even further at sea with this tangential comment, Nathan could only nod. "Yes. Lorne's a teacher in Nanaimo, Greg runs a greenhouse mid-Island, and Lyle is in Tofino. He's a surf instructor." That sounded better than beach bum. It wasn't the career he'd dreamed of for his youngest son, but Lyle had time to sort out his life. He didn't think Melanie had dropped in to talk about his parental worries, though. "What has that to do with the price of peanuts?"

Melanie grinned. "I intend to keep my job for a while longer yet. But the Regional Manager for Vancouver Island has been posted."

He raised his eyebrows in surprise. "And you thought of me?"

"Not that I want to lose you, but it seems a great fit. You'd be near your boys and get the promotion you deserve. Because you do deserve it, Nathan." Melanie expression was serious. "You're one of the best salespeople we've ever had, and you're a great mentor. I think you'd make an excellent manager."

His heart thudded heavily. It *did* sound like a perfect match, at least on paper.

But what about Helen?

He'd thought of her off and on throughout the day—her scent, the sounds she made when he caressed her, the softness of her skin.

He wished he knew what had prompted her impulsive invitation. Because it had been impulsive, as his acceptance had been. If they'd been rational adults, they would have talked about it first, discussed what it might mean—or not mean—to each of them. Not blazed their way into bed like two virgin teenagers.

On occasion over the years, he had dreamed of what might happen if he had the chance to explore his desire for her, but he had never thought past the actual deed. After all, it had just been a fantasy. But now the fantasy had come true, and he wanted to repeat it.

Not that Helen had given any indication she wanted the same, as evidenced by the way she'd scrambled out of bed. If anything, she'd acted as if she regretted their actions.

And now Melanie was dangling his ultimate career goal in front of him. He'd already lost one promotion because of a relationship. Would pursuing something with Helen put it all at risk again?

Melanie was waiting patiently for his reply, and he hurried to fill the silence. "Thanks for saying so. It means a lot. Do you really think I should apply?" He swivelled his chair. "I'm fifty-five years old. They probably want someone younger."

Melanie, only a year older than him, scoffed. "You're just a baby." Planting her feet on the floor, she speared him with a glare. "Wait a minute. You're not thinking of *retiring,* are you?" She spit out the word like it had a bad taste.

"No. Not for a while yet. But I bet you're not the only one wondering the same thing. Why would they invest in me if they think I'll be gone soon?"

She relaxed, pursing her lips dismissively. "Tell them the truth—that you plan on sticking around. And I know something else that will prove you're serious."

He knew instantly what she meant. "The Mount Morgan account?"

She nodded. "The Mount Morgan account. If you can wrap that up before your interview, you're practically a shoo-in. NIS has been trying to land that contract for years. The account exec who does will be the golden child."

Mount Morgan Mining was an international firm that operated a huge copper and gold mine a few hours north of Prince George. It had been on another salesperson's list for years, but Melanie had recently re-evaluated all accounts and it had landed on Nathan's plate. He'd been putting out cautious feelers, but his thoughtful, deliberate approach would have to slip into high gear if he wanted to lock it down anytime soon. "When does the posting for the promotion close?"

"The end of the month. Interviews will be scheduled immediately after. So, you have about two weeks." She slapped her hands on her knees and stood up. "If anyone can close Mount Morgan, Nathan, it's you."

A flare of excitement kindled. He loved his job, and while he was certainly making plans for retirement, he couldn't see himself twiddling his thumbs around the house for a decade yet. He still had time to make his mark. He'd always thought it would be here in his hometown, but maybe that had been short-sighted.

Yet he couldn't shake his unease whenever he thought of Helen.

Chapter Five

Helen poured herself a glass of wine and stepped out onto her back deck. Megan and Nora had just left, and as much as Helen adored her granddaughter, peace and quiet and alcohol were always welcome after dealing with the little girl's abundant energy all day.

She lowered herself into the all-weather wicker patio chair, sinking onto its deep foam cushion with a grateful sigh. Resting her bare feet on the low table the furniture was grouped around, she grinned at the pedicure Nora had given her. A different colour adorned each toe, and there was as much polish on her skin as on the nails, but it was beautiful to Helen's eyes.

It had been easy to ignore thoughts of next week's biopsy while she'd been distracted by Nora's rapid chatter and vibrant imagination. But the moment she let her guard down the anxiety swept in. Helen had always prided herself on not worrying about things that couldn't be changed. Summoning that serenity had been challenging the last couple of days.

The opening bars of the Swedish national anthem sounded from the kitchen, where she'd left her cell phone. With a groan she rose to her feet, hips and back complaining, and went to answer.

Sven Wiebe, owner of Golden Dragon Tattoos,

never called for social reasons. She wondered idly what the matter could be as she swiped to connect. "Hi, Sven."

"We're gonna do it." His gruff, gravelly voice rumbled through the speaker.

She sighed. "Do what, Sven?" Roundabout conversations were the norm with her boss.

"Go to Thailand. India and me. We leave in a month."

India was another part-time receptionist at Golden Dragon, and also Sven's on-again-off-again girlfriend. They appeared to be on-again. Helen wasn't sure their turbulent relationship would survive the flight to Bangkok, let alone months spent in close proximity, but that wasn't her place to say. "Good for you. You deserve a vacation. How long will you be gone?" He hadn't taken more than a long weekend in the two years Helen had worked for him.

"That's the thing. We don't know."

Helen frowned. "What does that mean?"

"Me and India, we don't want to be tied down with a return date."

"Oh, I see." That sounded very Sven-influenced-by-India, but she could handle that curveball. "Do you want me to manage Golden Dragon while you're gone?"

"No."

She stiffened at his uncompromising reply. She thought they'd built a solid professional relationship. If he didn't think she could keep the business afloat during his absence—

"I want you to buy it." Sven's words sliced like a sharpened blade through her disgruntled thoughts.

She'd left her wineglass outside and could see it from where she stood. Nope, still full. She wasn't drunk then. "Come again?"

"I'm selling Golden Dragon. Wanted you to have first crack at it."

Several minutes later, Helen staggered out and collapsed on the outdoor sofa once again, feeling rather as if she'd been run over by a bulldozer. Sven had finally agreed to discuss his harebrained idea the next day, when she would be at the shop, though he hadn't been happy about the delay.

Helen Mansfield, high school art teacher turned tattoo parlor owner. She buried her nose in her as-yet-untouched wineglass and snorted. Aaron would have been laughing his ass off. And telling her to go for it.

She could afford it, based on the asking price Sven had mentioned. She and Aaron had made wise investments, and with her pension and Aaron's life insurance she was nicely set. It was an established business, and she was a reasonably intelligent woman, so the risk would be acceptable.

I could own my own business. It wasn't something she'd ever thought of, but now she had, the challenge tickled at her, made her blood race. But how could she make such a momentous decision with the threat of cancer looming? She was under no illusions as to the devastating effects treatment could have on her stamina. She shouldn't even consider the idea.

Yet she couldn't stop thinking about it.

A gritty grating sound drew her attention to the yard next door. The floor of the deck was about level with the top of the fences separating her home from the houses on either side, so years ago Aaron had installed lattice on top of the railings for additional privacy. It didn't obscure her view so much that she couldn't identify Nathan as he stepped out onto his patio, a stemless wineglass in hand.

Helen shrank down in her seat and immediately realized how ridiculous that was. Before today, she would have hallooed cheerily across the space and invited him to bring his drink over. They might have discussed Sven's offer—minus the cancer issue, of course—maybe even had a pickup dinner together.

But they'd had sex, and now she was so self-conscious she could combust. That was only one reason for the heat suffusing her veins, though.

She wanted to be with him again, naked and sweaty and gasping. What she'd intended to be a one-time event had stirred longings she'd buried deep inside, and now those longings were scraping at her nerves, demanding to be fed.

He stood hipshot and relaxed at the edge of the cement pad that jutted out into the grassy expanse of lawn, sipping his drink. He wore work clothes—light-coloured slacks and a discreetly patterned dress shirt. He'd unbuttoned the long sleeves and rolled them back on his forearms, probably in deference to the heat still shimmering off the patio. He rarely wore a tie to the office and, if he had today, he'd already removed it, the collar framing his throat casually loose.

A bubble of desire tickled her belly and Helen gulped her wine to ease her dry mouth. She hadn't expected this lingering attraction and needed to rein it in. No matter how much she might want to repeat their encounter, she couldn't do so in good conscience, not with what was looming over her.

Before she could look away, Nathan turned, lifted his chin, and made eye contact through the lattice. His face lit in his familiar grin and then faltered. Maybe she wasn't the only one wondering how their relationship had changed after last night. Suppressing an absurd urge to duck even lower, she lifted one hand and waggled her fingers in a feeble greeting.

"Hey." He raised his glass, golden liquid glowing in the sunlight. "Do you mind if I come over?"

It had been a long time since Nathan had asked if

it was okay to drop in. The two couples and their kids had been in and out of each other's houses without ceremony for decades. The polite question highlighted the shift between them.

She cleared her throat. "Of course not."

He nodded and disappeared inside. She waited, irritatingly breathless with unwanted anticipation, until he reappeared a minute later, emerging from the narrow space between her house and the fence that led to the front yard. The silver in his hair glinted as he circled the deck and climbed the flight of stairs to join her.

Nathan hadn't been able to prevent a bloom of pleasure when he'd seen Helen on her deck, though it had been quickly replaced with an unwelcome uncertainty.

Awkward emotions had had no place in his other two affairs. With those women, he'd been looking for short-term companionship, and yes, sex. Helen was...different. He had felt something for her, something deeper than friendship, warmer than desire, even before they'd made love. But now, if he wanted to explore what they might have together, he'd have to reject his second—and probably last—chance at promotion. There was no way to have both, especially with the move his new job would require.

She watched with a wary expression as he climbed the stairs to her deck. He didn't blame her for feeling ill at ease. They'd upset the traditional balance of their relationship. It didn't matter that they'd known each other for decades—last night had changed everything.

His stomach knotted with unaccustomed nerves as he took a seat on the sofa, knowing they had to talk. He decided to ease into the conversation with a safe question.

"How was your day?" He knew Helen's schedule as well as he knew his own. She stared blankly for a moment, and then smiled, her tense shoulders relaxing. Spending time with her granddaughter always put her in a good mood.

"It was great. Nora and I went to the water park in the morning and then after lunch she gave me a pedicure." She raised one foot and pointed her toes so he could admire the sparkling rainbow of colours.

He let his gaze trail up her calf, past her knee, to the smooth thigh bared by her short skirt. Now he knew exactly how satiny her skin was, what the plump folds between her legs tasted like...

His wandering thoughts brought unexpected clarification. While he would have to spend every available hour between now and the end of the month closing the Mount Morgan deal to secure his promotion, he was sure he could carve out time for Helen. Her reaction last night had indicated she wasn't looking for anything long-term. Maybe this was exactly what she *was* looking for.

He worked saliva into his dry mouth. "Very nice. She has a talent."

Amusement gleamed in her bright eyes. "How about you? How was your day?"

"Good, good." His gut—and years of negotiations—told him to hold back the news about the Vancouver Island job for now. If she seemed hesitant at what he was about to propose, he could sweeten the pot by mentioning his possible departure.

Leaning forward, he rested his elbows on his knees while cupping his empty glass in both hands and met Helen's gaze. "I can't stop thinking of you, of what we did together. I admit, I was surprised at first. But I am very glad you asked me."

Helen's focus flittered away and a flush rose on her cheeks. "I enjoyed it, too."

"I'd like to do it again." *That* got her attention, as

he'd intended. Her body stilled, all but for a rapid pulse beating in her neck. "Tonight, if you're amenable."

She dropped her feet to the floor and straightened in her seat, a deep frown creasing her brow. "I don't think that's a good idea."

He hadn't expected her to fling herself into his lap, but he had thought she'd be a little more open to the idea. "Tonight? Or ever?"

"Ever."

He should have left it at that. But he had seen her eyes drift down his body before flicking shyly away. One more try wouldn't hurt.

With the ease of long habit, he slipped into bargaining mode. "Can you explain why not? You said you enjoyed yourself, and I know I did. I also got the impression you don't want anything too serious, and neither do I. If you're worried being lovers might—"

She cut him off before he could promise not to let sex ruin their friendship. "Lovers?" Her mouth pressed into a thin line. "Exactly what did you think last night was all about, Nathan?"

Taken aback, he asked with wary caution, "What did *you* think it was?"

"I didn't mean to mislead you. I'm not looking for a—a lover, either short- or long-term. I was given disturbing news yesterday and was feeling lonely, vulnerable. I turned to you because I knew you wouldn't take advantage of that."

So, something *had* been bothering her. He should have pressed her then, not let her distract him with passion. He wouldn't let her get away with it a second time. "What disturbing news, Helen?"

"Nothing that affects you."

"The hell it doesn't." He placed his wine glass on the table with a sharp crack and Helen flinched. "You're my friend, first and foremost. You can't say something like that and not explain yourself."

She lifted her chin. "Just because we slept together doesn't mean you can start making demands."

"It has nothing to do with having slept together." Although maybe it did. He had never felt this protective of Helen before. But joining their bodies had obviously ignited his primitive impulses. He rose and took a seat beside her on the couch. Her eyes widened as he gripped her hand in both of his. "I care for you, Helen. You have to know that. And I'm sure whatever I'm imagining is worse than the truth. So put me out of my misery. What's going on?"

"I can't tell you."

Tears welled in her eyes and horror gripped him. The only time he'd seen Helen cry was at Aaron's funeral. "Is it Megan? Is everything okay with her?" His lungs locked. "Or Nora? Tell me this has nothing to do with Nora."

Helen shook her head in rapid, jerky movements. Relief did nothing to dull the creep of fear down his spine. "It's you then." He became aware his grasp of her hands was so tight he could feel her bones rubbing together and immediately relaxed his muscles. "For god's sake, Helen. Tell me."

She searched his face for interminable seconds, and then her shoulders slumped in defeat. "I might have breast cancer."

Chapter Six

Helen had known that no matter when she told Nathan, he would be shocked by her announcement, given Wanda's fatal battle with the disease. Even as he'd gently badgered her, she'd had every intention of holding her secret close. But his shocked, desperate expression when he thought her worries might be for Megan or Nora had made it obvious she couldn't prevaricate any longer.

He had yet to respond to her statement. The colour had leached from his cheeks and his pale blue eyes were flat and cold as ice on a mountain lake. He hadn't moved and his hands still clasped hers, but they were inert, motionless.

When he made no attempt to speak a wave of panic, dizzy and wild, swept through her. She tugged her fingers from his limp grip and twisted them together.

She'd known he'd be upset. But what if he couldn't handle it? What if he broke off their relationship completely? She hadn't even *considered* that possibility.

"Nothing's for sure yet." Her lips were dry, her tongue too big for her mouth. "I went in for an ultrasound after my annual mammogram revealed an area of concern. It confirmed a mass in my right breast. I have a biopsy scheduled for a week today. I should have the results seven to ten days after that."

Nathan closed his eyes, as if unable to bear the sight of her, and her panic grew. While she couldn't gamble on being his lover, she also couldn't lose his friendship—didn't know if she could make it through the weeks until her fate was determined without his support.

Nathan had become indispensable in her life in such tiny increments she hadn't noticed the change. Now she had blurted out the one thing that could sever their friendship forever.

A flare of fury pierced her anxiety. It was his own fault she'd told him. If he hadn't poked and prodded, had accepted her rejection, everything would have been fine.

He sat there, eyes shut, silent. *Well, screw you, then.*

"I'm sure it's nothing." She intended her tone to be brisk and light, but the angry buzzing in her ears made it hard to hear herself. "I have very dense breasts, and it's probably a benign cyst. I wasn't going to tell anyone until I had more details. Which means Megan doesn't know, so you'll have to keep this to yourself. I don't want to worry her unnecessarily."

He raised his eyelids, and his fierce look sent the breath rushing from her lungs. "You haven't even told your *daughter*? Your *doctor* daughter? Are you some sort of superwoman that you can handle this all on your own?"

She bristled at his censure. "I don't even know if there's anything *to* handle. The results are weeks away yet. There will be plenty of time to figure things out after it's confirmed to be c-cancer." Horrified she'd stumbled over the dreaded word, she jutted her chin and repeated it defiantly. "And even if it is cancer, the biopsy will remove the entire lump, so that will be the end of it."

"That's what Wanda thought, too," Nathan said bitterly.

The rollercoaster of her emotions took a deep, spinning dive. Helen jumped to her feet and glared down at him. "I don't need this negative energy right now. Maybe you should go."

Nathan's hollow, pale look was eaten up by a wildness that made her lean away. Red flags burned his cheekbones, and he looked as angry as she'd ever seen him. "*This* is what last night was about? You're afraid you're dying and wanted one last fling?"

It was as if the air crystallized around her. *Dying*. She'd been avoiding that word, even in her thoughts. "Get out."

Nathan rose slowly, one hand outstretched. "I'm sorry. I didn't mean it. You're not dying. Of course you're not."

"I told you. I don't need any more negativity right now." She bit back more recriminations. He wasn't wrong about her reasons for sleeping with him. "Maybe I did want one last fling. What's so bad about that? I was feeling alone and frightened. Breast cancer runs in my family, you know that. If I have it, it will be a severe, painful battle. I want to wring every last ounce of enjoyment out of life I can, starting now. And if you can't support me in that—" She shrugged, hoping he couldn't see the effort it cost her to appear unconcerned, unafraid.

She faced him, shoulders squared, separated by the air between them and a gulf of experience so wide and painful it echoed.

"I need to think." Nathan sidled out from between the sofa and the table. "I need to decide what this means." He headed for the stairs. "Goodbye, Helen."

Ice closed around her heart at the finality of his words.

Golden Dragon Tattoo Parlor was tucked into an awkward corner of a small strip mall a ten-minute drive from Helen's house. Thursday morning, she pulled into a slot in the rear parking lot and realized she didn't remember anything between backing out of her driveway and turning off the ignition.

That wasn't good. Not good at all. More than twelve hours after Nathan's rejection and she was still swirling in a maelstrom of panic and sorrow and regret. And the discussion she and Sven needed to have this morning didn't bode well for regaining her balance.

She entered the shop and headed to the front counter. Even this early in the day, she welcomed the air-conditioned comfort, as the heat wave showed no signs of abating. Sven and Jamie, his apprentice, usually arrived a few minutes before opening at nine o'clock, so she had the next half hour or so to ensure everything was ready—and clear her mind of the debacle with Nathan. The routine was soothing, and she slipped into it with relief.

After Aaron's death, she'd been desperate to fill her achingly empty days. Looking after Nora once a week helped but wasn't enough. Starting the Silverberry Book Club had occupied a few more hours, but she was still left with too much free time. Time in which to think of all she'd had, all she'd lost, and the years left to endure. When she'd seen the post searching for a receptionist at Golden Dragon, she had applied on a whim and never regretted it.

Even if the biopsy wasn't casting its threatening shadow, though, deciding to buy a business wasn't something a sane person did without careful thought. While she was confident she could manage the shop for a short period, *owning* it was something else all together. And she would never be able to match Sven for skill. He had bullied her into learning how to do single colour tattoos, declaring her art background was one of the reasons he'd hired her, and she'd practiced on oranges for months until she'd met his high standards. But there was no way she would ever compare to Sven, who was a true artist, inspired and dramatic and talented. Jamie was the one being groomed to replace him, but they still had a way to go.

Most importantly, though, she couldn't even *think* about buying until after her biopsy results were in. Sven would just have to accept the delay.

As she sorted the colourful ink used in the more elaborate designs, she reviewed the day's appointments in her head. Large tattoos took hours—and sometimes multiple visits—to create, so she knew many of Golden Dragon's clients well because of the amount of time they spent in the chair. It also seemed that, for most people, one tattoo wasn't enough, so return clients were plentiful.

Even she fell into that category. A vision of the stunned, lustful look on Nathan's face when he'd seen her tattoos for the first-time riffled heat down her spine. She shoved it aside. The chances of seeing that expression again had evaporated like mist on water.

She was still a little shocked she'd allow Sven to badger and bully her into getting the designs. His argument had been she should know how it felt so she could give better advice. When she'd finally agreed, he'd inked the rose on her hip. It had been Aaron's favourite flower. A few weeks later she'd asked for the heart on her upper breast.

At the time, she hadn't been exactly sure why she'd had it done but had come to realize it was a form of reparation. Though she still believed she'd done the right thing, motherhood and maturity had given her an understanding of her mother she hadn't had as a teenager.

While checking the sterilization equipment was working properly and wiping down the chairs and beds with sanitizing spray, she contemplated a new irony. The tattoo was on the breast with the lump—the breast now trying to kill her. Maybe she could spin that into a positive. Was it possible her mother's spirit would ensure the lump was benign? It was a nice thought, but she wouldn't hold her breath.

The back door opened and closed, and she shook off past resentment to prepare for present tribulations. "Good morning," she called.

Her answer was the thud of a heavy bag being tossed on the floor and an unintelligible grunt—the latter a sign Sven was in an approachable mood. It was the mornings when he shouted "What the hell's good about it?" that she had to worry his creative temper was flaring. Given the discussion she'd promised they'd have—and the question she needed to ask—his subdued response was the best she could hope for.

A moment later, he emerged from the hall leading from the treatment rooms. As befitted his first name, he was a blond giant with biceps that bulged from the weight training he did every morning. Those same biceps were covered in intricately inked designs, a few tendrils of which wound up his shoulders to circle his neck.

He planted his palms on the counter and stared at her, eyes narrowed. "So, what's it going to be? You in or you out?"

It had taken a few weeks to get used to his intimidating attitude, but she knew now it was a by-product of his menacing size, gruff voice, and abrupt manner, and not a warning sign of an aggressive personality. "Aren't you being hasty, deciding to sell because you want to travel for a while? Wouldn't it be better if I managed the place? You and India could wander to your heart's content and come back whenever you want, take up where you left off."

Sven held up his hands. The knuckles were gnarled, the fingers curled. "I'm too crippled to keep doing this work much longer. And no way in hell will I spend my days sitting up here making nicey-nice with clients. Jamie is doing amazing stuff and is ready to take over, even though they don't think so. It's time to push them out of the nest. That goes for you, too." He crossed his massive arms over his chest and scowled.

"I need some time." The yearning to say yes burned in her chest, but she'd already made one impulsive decision that week, asking Nathan to have sex, and look how that had turned out.

"Don't take too long about it. And don't chicken out." Sven frowned over her shoulder at the online calendar that kept track of all appointments. "Who have we got first?"

Helen's shoulders softened at his temporary—yet threatening—acceptance of the delay. "Daveed is in for the next stage of his sleeve. I've got you blocked off for four hours for that." It struck her suddenly that Sven had been cutting back on his work for a while. When she'd started, a full day of inking was the norm. Today's four hours was his max now. Maybe his decision to sell the business wasn't as impetuous as it seemed. "Jamie has a couple smaller tats this morning and is starting on Sierra's back this afternoon."

He grunted in acknowledgment. "You okay to handle walk-ins?"

"Sure." With precise movements, she lined up the edge of the photo album Sven used as a portfolio with the edge of the counter, and then bit the next bullet. "I can't work my usual days next week."

He loomed over her and his gaze lasered in on her face. "Why the hell not?"

"I'd rather not say." If he knew she might have cancer, he might renege on his offer, which would be a crushing disappointment. She *wanted* to take on that challenge—as long as she was healthy enough to handle it. She turned to face him, lifting her chin. "I haven't asked for a shift change the entire time I've been here. Surely you can accommodate me this once."

"You only work two goddamn days a week. A little notice would have been nice."

She didn't flinch at his bark. The only way to deal with a ferocious Sven was to bark right back. "I can do Monday and Tuesday for India if she can take my days."

"You're goddamn lucky she can."

Helen didn't bother asking how Sven was so certain of that. He could battle it out with India himself. Maybe they'd have a big blow-up fight and Sven would change his mind about leaving. Then she wouldn't have to decide about buying the shop. It wasn't relief she felt at that thought, though, but chagrin. "Okay. I'll take that as approval."

He narrowed his eyes. "Is this going to happen often?"

"No." It wasn't a total lie. She knew how debilitating invasive surgery and treatments could be, but if that were necessary, she'd do the right thing and give her notice so Sven could replace her. It would complicate his plans to escape to Thailand, but she couldn't think about that. Either way, she was going to miss his pugnaciousness and blazing talent. In the grand scheme of things, though, leaving Golden Dragon would be one of the smallest losses her future might hold.

Chapter Seven

Nathan left the boardroom at Mount Morgan Mining's Prince George offices with a hopeful glow burning in his chest. He'd had this meeting with the Specialist in Vendor Management and various other purchasing officials scheduled well before Melanie's announcement about the promotion, but the pressure to make it productive had definitely amped up. He was heartened that he'd been asked to prepare a substantial proposal and arranged to present it in one week. He'd offered to have the bid ready sooner, but the committee had held firm on their timeline. They had promised to make a decision within seven days of receiving the proposal, but that would be after the posting for the promotion closed. The best he could hope for was good news in time to announce it during his interview. While the delay rankled, he knew putting the package together would take up much of his free time as it was, so maybe it was a good thing.

Since he had nothing other than work to occupy his hours. Certainly not time spent in Helen's bed.

He was still reeling from her news, still processing the abrupt changes their relationship had gone through in the last few days. She was a good friend—maybe even his *best* friend—and having sex with her had broken a barrier in his heart he hadn't even known was there. To have a fatal illness rear its terrifying head again, barely a day later, left him staggering and off-balance.

While he didn't the same commitment to Helen as he had had to Wanda, the similarities were disturbing—a woman he cared for caught in the web of cancer just as a critical moment in his career. Assuring himself he didn't have to feel guilty if he put his job first this time hadn't eased his mind one bit.

He was barely out of the parking lot when his phone rang. It automatically connected to his SUV's handsfree system and his middle son's name appeared on the screen.

He connected the call. "Hi, Greg! How are you?"

"Doing good, Dad. Did I catch you at a bad time?"

"Just on my way back to the office, but I've got a minute." Mount Morgan's offices were in an industrial area on the south side of the Fraser River. Taking a left instead of the right that would lead him to the city centre, he drove a few metres down the gravel road that ran along the ridge above the river and pulled onto the shoulder. "What's up?"

"Lorne told me about the regional sales manager job."

"Ah." He'd known the news would get around soon but hadn't thought it would be this fast.

After fleeing from Helen last evening, Nathan had paced his house, unable to settle. Needing time to absorb her news, he had sought distraction by video chatting with his oldest son and two grandchildren. He hadn't meant to mention the possible promotion, but his subconscious had obviously had other plans, and once it slipped out there had been no taking it back.

"Don't get too excited. I haven't even put in my resume yet." Because he'd superstitiously decided to delay until after today's meeting with Mount Morgan. If things had gone completely sideways, he might have had to rethink his plans. With the glimmer of hope he'd been given, sending off his application was the first thing he'd do when he returned to his office.

"That's what Lorne said. After he told me, I talked with Lyle, and we're all on the same page. We want you to go for it, Dad. It would be so awesome if you were on the Island."

He was happy his sons wanted him nearby and felt guilty for giving the impression he was ambivalent about the promotion. He wasn't. He wanted it as much as he had five years ago, maybe even more since it would bring him closer to his boys.

It wasn't the first time the topic of Nathan uprooting from Prince George had been broached after Wanda's death, especially since Lyle had made the move to the Island last year. The two oldest were married and grandbabies were appearing with startling regularity, and while Nathan connected with them via text, phone, and video chat often, it wasn't the same as being there.

"It would be awesome, I agree. You know I'd love to see everyone more." Nathan stared blindly out the windshield. Power lines swooping from huge metal structures stretched across the wide, mud-coloured water, ruining the rustic setting, but it was an impressive view, nonetheless. He fell back on his usual excuse. "It's not that simple, though. Your grandparents are strong and healthy now, but that won't last forever. They're going to need more help at some point, and if I'm on the Island, I won't be available."

Greg replied with *his* usual rebuttal. "Auntie Dana and Uncle Mattieu will still be there. And it's only an hour's flight from Victoria to Prince George."

He wasn't wrong. Nathan's sister and her husband could be trusted to step up, and he knew his admitted reason was weak. "True, but—"

Greg cut him off. "Even if you don't get the

promotion, we think you should move. I'm sure you could find another job here if you wanted. Or you could retire, spend more time with the grandkids. And the weather is so much better here. You must be tired of shovelling snow by now."

Nathan paid Twin Rivers Landscape and Maintenance—another client of his—to clear his driveway and mow his lawn, but he knew what Greg meant. Watching the heat waves shimmering off the stretch of road before him, it was hard to believe that, in a few short months, frigid temperatures and blankets of snow would once again be the norm.

The thing was, Nathan's life was in Prince George. Not just his job and his parents, his friends and his history, but Helen, too. He couldn't mention her to his sons, though. He wouldn't know where to start if he tried to explain their relationship—not even *before* all that had happened in recent days.

After Aaron had died, he hadn't wanted to leave her to face her new reality alone, even for the pleasure of his sons' regular company, a chance to get to know his daughters-in-law better, and the joy of seeing his grandchildren more often. Looking back, he wondered if his subconscious had been considering the possibility of nurturing something deeper with Helen—something more than simple physical attraction.

But now she might have cancer. And Nathan didn't know if he was strong enough to stand by her side while she went through what she'd have to endure.

She deserved someone who could.

It was amazing what people said while in the tattoo chair. Helen concentrated on the infinity symbol she was inking on Lynn Kolmyn's inner wrist while listening to her talk of things her best friends probably didn't know.

"All I've ever wanted was a job I liked, a husband, a couple of kids. Then two weeks ago, my fiancé of seven years dumps me to chase a dream. And here I am, with no hint of husband or babies, and I'm thirty-eight years old. Thirty-eight! How did that happen?"

The blonde woman had entered Golden Dragon around four o'clock, setting the old-fashioned bell above the door jingling. She was an inch above average height and dressed with fashionable but casual elegance in slim dark jeans and a silk tank. Helen had recognized the nervous, vaguely lost look of a tattoo virgin and had slipped into her usual patter. Lynn had been the first walk-in that day, and Helen was grateful finally to have something to occupy her other than thoughts of next week's biopsy. Together they'd flipped through Sven's portfolio, and Lynn had decided on the interlinking loops, balking only a moment or two when Helen said it could be done immediately.

"Life has a way of slipping by when we're not paying attention. That's why we have to grab *what* we can *when* we can." Helen dabbed with a gauze pad to remove the tiny dot of blood that had welled and considered the truth of what she'd said. If she wanted to grab her own opportunity and take on Golden Dragon, she might have to break her unwritten rule and ask for help. Even if she did have cancer, it didn't have to mean putting her entire life on hold. She'd just have to get creative about it.

"I was paying attention. I had it all figured out. I established my career, found a good man, got engaged." Lynn hissed in a breath as Helen set the tattoo machine to her flesh for the final touch. "Then it all fell apart, and now my biological clock is ticking so loudly I can't sleep at night. I'm a cliché, I know."

"That doesn't make what you are feeling any less

valid." Helen sat back. "There. What do you think?"

Lynn studied her wrist with a bemused air, twisting it back and forth to see the design from all angles. "I really must be having a crisis. I only came to the plaza to pick up my dry cleaning, and the next thing I know I'm in here. But I like it."

"Great." Helen rose from her stool. "Feel free to hang out for a bit while I tidy up. Some people get a little light-headed after being poked with a needle for an hour."

She busied herself putting away her equipment while Lynn sat quietly in the chair. The younger woman's expression was pensive, and Helen didn't think her thoughts had anything to do with the tattoo she'd just received.

Lynn's words resonated with Helen. Her life had also come to an unexpected crossroads. She, too, might be running out of time to do things she'd planned. And while she'd been desperately lonely after Aaron died, she'd come to appreciate her solitude.

Which didn't mean she wanted to be *alone*. Too bad she'd screwed up her chances of having Nathan be the one by her side.

As Lynn rose from the seat and took her purse from the hook on the door, Helen gave into impulse. "Feel free to say no, but I run the Silverberry Book Club. We meet once a month, have drinks, snacks, talk about books. Would you like to come? Maybe meet new people?"

Lynn gave her a startled glance, and then hope gleamed in her eyes. "Do you mean that? You don't even know me."

"Our next meeting is mid-August." Helen's heart fluttered. By then she'd know whether she had cancer or not. She wasn't sure whether she wanted time to speed up or slow down. "It will be at the cabin one of our members has on Cluculz Lake. Given how hot this summer has been, we thought we would mix business with pleasure, so to speak." Nathan was the member in question. She assumed he wouldn't withdraw his invitation regardless of what had happened between them. He wouldn't do that to the club.

Lynn's smile lit up her rather sober face, and Helen blinked at the transformation. "That sounds great. Thank you for inviting me."

She smiled back. "Wonderful! I'll text you the directions and which book we'll be discussing. So glad to have you join us."

Chapter Eight

The heat wave continued during the next few days.

And so did the deep freeze between Helen and Nathan.

This was exactly the reason she hadn't intended to tell anyone. Cancer changed everything, and while Helen told herself dealing with it on her own was what she'd wanted, what she'd planned all along, it still hurt. She would never have insisted on his undivided attention, as her mother had demanded of her, but since he had badgered her into telling him, the least he could have done was offer encouragement.

Not that she blamed him. She had deserted her own mother, after all. Why should she deserve anything different from anyone else?

Over the last lonely while, though, she had come to realize how much she depended on Nathan's steadfast companionship. The gaping hole it gouged in her life was a chasm she didn't know how to fill.

When the knock sounded on her door at ten o'clock Sunday morning, the last person she expected to see was Nathan. Yet there he was, standing cool and confident on her front step. She swallowed back an exclamation of relief and joy, the sensation of *rightness* blossoming in her chest both welcome and terrifying.

The half-smile curving his lips faded as his gaze swept down and up her body. "I'm sorry. I shouldn't have assumed you'd still come golfing with me."

Confused, she looked down at the maxi-dress sweeping her bare feet, and then back to Nathan. "Golfing?" Her eyes widened as his meaning clicked. "The Mount Morgan Mining Charity Tournament. That's today?"

He nodded while the corners of his mouth pinched. "I'm sorry," he repeated, taking a step back. "I'll go on my own. It's not a problem."

"No!" Now he was here, she wasn't going to let him get away. The drive to the golf course was the perfect opportunity to try and mend things between them. She couldn't lose her best friend, not yet, not now. "It totally escaped me, that's all. I can be ready in a minute."

"Don't come if it's going to be awkward."

She smiled with slightly manic brightness to offset his grim tone. "It won't. I'll be right there. My clubs are in the garage. Do you mind getting them for me? You know the code to open the door." She raced up the short flight of steps leading to the main floor and her bedroom.

Helen dragged off her dress and wriggled into a sports bra, a white sleeveless collared shirt and a hot-pink athletic skort. She hustled out of the house as Nathan loaded her clubs on their three-wheeled cart into the back of his SUV. He glanced over and without comment rounded the vehicle to the driver's door. In matching silence, she climbed in beside him and latched her seatbelt as he reversed onto the street.

She waited in a welter of mingled impatience and reluctance until he'd navigated out of their neighbourhood. The course hosting the tournament was about twenty minutes away. She hoped it would be long enough to set things right.

"I'm sorry I upset you." She was thankful he had

to keep his eyes on the road. It gave her an excuse to avoid looking at him. "I didn't intend to mention the biopsy at all, but I couldn't *not* tell you, not after you..." She didn't want to make things worse by pointing out he had insisted, rather forcefully.

He had no trouble filling in the blank. "Wouldn't take no for an answer? You have nothing to be sorry about, Helen. I should have respected your privacy."

"Well, yes." *Too late for that, now.*

Nathan slowed as the road swept around a wide, arching curve and under the twin double-lane bridges that spanned the Fraser River flowing at her right. "I'm sorry I reacted the way I did. But your refusal to tell me made me imagine all sorts of horrors. Not that I imagined this." He sighed. "I do wish you'd told me before..."

It was her turn to fill in the blank. "Before we had sex. I know. I should have been honest. But I never intended it to go further than one night. I was only thinking of myself, and that wasn't fair to you. I should have considered what you might think it meant." She was still a little astonished he had wanted to be with her again. Flattered, but astonished.

"Helen."

She clasped her damp palms together and looked at him, chin raised. For the moment he allowed his attention to waver from the street, his gaze was warm, direct, and rueful. When he turned away, she shuddered from a searing sense of loss.

"I wasn't angry you rejected my offer of an affair," he said. "My reaction had nothing to do with that. I *am* angry you didn't trust me with your news. And I am worried about *you*. For what you might have to go through. And what that might mean for us."

Unwanted hope flared at his words. She didn't want—*couldn't* want—their relationship to become an *us*. But he wouldn't say something like that if he wasn't willing to maintain their friendship.

"I still want you in my life, if you can bear it. But I'm not in the right mental place to start a new relationship." Helen wiggled her fingers in a helpless gesture. "That night I needed...I just *needed*. And you were there."

A low growl emanated from the driver's seat and Helen's eyes flew wide. "Oh! I didn't mean it that way!" Burying her head in her hands, she spoke through muffling fingers. "I am trying to fix things, and I keep making them worse."

Hearing Helen butcher her unnecessary apology tickled Nathan in a black, ironic way. It appeased a tiny, selfish need to see her as discombobulated as he was.

Lifting one hand off the steering wheel, he gently gripped her wrist and tugged. "It's okay, Helen. I'm not insulted, if that's what you're thinking."

She dropped her hands into her lap and straightened from her hunched position. "How could you not be? I basically said any faceless stranger would have done that night."

Thinking of Helen with another man made him queasy. He didn't want to examine why. "You didn't mean it that way. Don't you remember what you said last Wednesday?" He could feel her gaze on his profile, bright and intense. "You asked me because you knew I wouldn't take advantage of you. So not any man would have done, right?"

For several seconds, the only noise in the cabin of the vehicle was the hum of the tires and whoosh of the air conditioner. Then Helen released a soft exhalation. "You're right. Sorry again. I'm not usually so melodramatic."

"It's okay." He patted her thigh in what he hoped was a friendly, unloverlike gesture. "We're good?"

"We're good."

As if drained by the conversation, Helen leaned back in her seat and stared out her window. The silence gave him time to recalibrate his own emotions and get ready for the day ahead.

The Mount Morgan Mining Charity Golf Tournament was a major fundraising event for the local hospital, drawing in reigning and would-be politicians, professional athletes, powerful businesspeople, and the general public. When he'd signed up weeks ago, he had seen it as a way to get to know the company's ethics, meet some of the staff in a casual, relaxed setting. Since his meeting on Thursday, every interaction now had a deeper, more intense repercussion. One wrong word could cast a black cloud on his presentation—or, more positively, a good impression could pave the way to accepting his proposal and launching him into his promotion.

A promotion Helen knew nothing about yet.

He slid her a sideways glance. He'd been relieved when she hadn't ducked out of the tournament, taking it as a sign she was willing to forgive his boorish behaviour. Now he realized it was because she'd completely forgotten about it. And here they were, just learning how to be comfortable with each other again, and he had to rock the boat by telling her he might be leaving town.

He had to do it, though. If they hadn't been at odds recently, she would already know. And as thankful as he was that they'd managed to work past the conflicts of the last few days, she couldn't stay in ignorance any longer, no matter what her reaction might be.

He made the last turn into the golf course and negotiated the parking lot, buzzing with golfers, carts, and vehicles, and searched for a free space. Spying an open slot, he slipped his SUV in. Before he could draw breath to make his revelation, Helen escaped the cab, opening the hatch practically before the engine died.

Her golf clubs rattled as she dragged them out. In the rear-view mirror he watched as she unfolded the collapsible cart and dug her shoes out of one of the bag's zippered pockets, her face set and weary.

They may have patched the hole between them, but it didn't look like Helen was quite ready to go back to their old easy habits, yet. That didn't bode well for what had to come next.

Telling himself not to be a coward, he rounded the rear of the SUV and took out his own clubs. Helen sat on the bumper and slipped out of her sandals, keeping her face averted. "There's something I need to tell you, Helen." He unzipped a pocket on his golf bag and drew out his glove.

She stiffened and flicked him a glance from the corner of her eye. "Can we talk about whatever it is later?" she said, keeping her body angled away. "I've had enough drama for one day."

He wished he could give her a respite, but it had to be now. "It has to do with the golf tournament."

She tied her right shoe, set that foot on the ground, and raised her left. "Fine."

"A position has come open in the Vancouver Island office of NIS. Regional Sales Manager." He cleared his throat and fidgeted with his glove. "I have applied."

Helen's fingers fumbled on the laces of her shoe, thoughts tumbling in her brain, fighting for supremacy.

She couldn't imagine her world without Nathan nearby. But his boys lived on the Island. And he'd wanted a management job for a long time. It would be a great move for him, personally and professionally.

Forcing a smile onto her face, she dragged her gaze to meet his. "Best of luck." The words choked her, but a good friend would say them. "I know you wanted that other position—" She broke off. Maybe she shouldn't remind him of the opportunities he'd missed due to Wanda's illness.

He didn't need her to finish her thought, though. "Yes. This is probably my last kick at the can. I'm happy doing what I'm doing, but it would be nice to round off my career in a management position. And with the boys and my grandchildren there..." He raised a shoulder expressively.

"It sounds perfect for you." Oddly, Nathan's body language wasn't reflecting the excitement she had expected. "It is perfect, isn't it? What do you think, Nathan?"

He tucked his glove in his back pocket, took out his golf shoes and loosened the laces. "So much has happened in the last few days. You and me, your cancer, this new job. I don't know what to think."

"You have to go for it. You'd hate yourself if you didn't." She laid her hand on his, stilling his movements. Nathan stared at it. "If you're feeling guilty about applying, don't. Whatever is going on in my life has nothing to do with this." Now she felt even worse for giving in to Nathan's exhortations to tell what was on her mind. If he lost this promotion because of her, she'd—well, she didn't know what she'd do, but she knew she would feel awful.

He shook his head, rather like a horse ridding itself of pesky flies. "The posting closes at the end of the month. This is where the golf tournament comes in. Melanie—you remember my boss, Melanie?" At Helen's confirming nod he went on. "Melanie thinks I'm sure to get the promotion if I can close a sale with Mount Morgan."

The lightbulb went on in Helen's brain. No wonder he'd insisted on telling her this news right now. She straightened her shoulders. "So, you need to make a good impression today. What can I do to help?"

Chapter Nine

Helen and Nathan were partnered with two women from the human resources department at Mount Morgan. She assumed he would have rather golfed with people that held more clout in the company, but he didn't let his disappointment show, and the foursome whack-thunked their way around the neatly groomed par three in cheerful comradery.

Nathan had assured her she didn't need to do anything other than be herself—cheerful, outgoing, and friendly. It was easier said than done, as she was still in turmoil over his news, but as the day went on she wore her hostess role with less difficulty.

They finished their round, and the foursome split up amicably. Most of the money at these charitable events was raised during the dinner and auctions held after all the golfers were back at the clubhouse, so there was still time for Nathan to make the connections he sought. Helen stayed by his side as he moved smoothly through the crowd chatting with other participants while they waited for the final stragglers to wander in.

A bright, chipper voice broke through the chatter. "Mrs. Mansfield! Is that you?"

Helen swung to her left and a wide smile lifted her cheeks. "Natalie! How are you? It's been ages!" She wrapped the younger dark-haired woman in her arms, rocking her back and forth enthusiastically. "What are you doing here?"

"I'm with Oliver O'Keefe." Natalie tossed a thumb over her shoulder and Helen's gaze followed the gesture. She recognized the tall man with heavy brows and broad shoulders as a local lawyer with political aspirations. Standing with O'Keefe was a sleek, blonde woman and two middle-aged men. All four wore casual golf clothes, but there was something in the stiffness of their stances that shouted they'd feel more comfortable in suits and ties.

Natalie leaned in conspiratorially. "It's not common knowledge, but the current Member of the Legislative Assembly for Prince George North won't be running in the next election. Oliver is going for the nomination."

"And you're helping run his campaign." By profession, Natalie was a librarian at the local public library, and while she had just turned thirty—she was the same age as Megan—Helen knew she'd been active politically, though always behind the scenes, for years.

"Yes. It's an amazing opportunity. For him and me." Natalie's gaze slid from Helen to Nathan and her eyebrows quirked. "Have we met? You seem familiar."

"This is Nathan Spieth, my"—Helen stumbled as she recalled their current undefined status and went with what was the easiest truth—"neighbour. Nathan, do you remember Natalie Minton? She and Megan met in university, and she lived with us for several months her final year."

"Of course. Nice to see you again, Natalie." Nathan shook her hand.

A blush rose on Natalie cheeks. "It's Panwar, actually. Natalie Panwar. I got married a few weeks ago."

Helen squealed and pulled Natalie into a second hug. "What? I hadn't heard that! I'll have to give

Megan what for."

"Megan doesn't know, either. It all happened rather fast."

"Is your husband here? I'd love to meet him."

Natalie's eyes went blank, and she rolled her shoulders as if shrugging off a burden. "No. He had other commitments today."

Helen wondered uneasily if the hurried wedding had a shaky foundation. She had to be reading more into Natalie's reaction than it deserved. "Well, pass on my congratulations and all the best to you both. So, who's that with your candidate?"

Natalie's relief at the change in subject only increased Helen's concern. "The woman is his wife, Aubrey Windt. The men are big wigs from the sponsor, Mount Morgan. The taller one is the CFO, Stanley Allbright. The other is Vice-President of Operations, Julius Thames."

Nathan, who'd been quiet yet attentive throughout the conversation, gave a quiet grunt. With mingled elation and sadness, Helen realized this was her chance to do something concrete to help.

"Would you mind introducing us?" she asked Natalie. "Nathan is an account executive at Nechako Industrial Supply and Mount Morgan is a client of his. I'm sure he'd appreciate it."

"Don't let Helen put you on the spot." Helen was sure she heard more than a hint of longing in his calm, deep voice. This was exactly the opportunity he'd been looking for all day. And as much as she would hate—absolutely *hate*—if he moved away, she couldn't stand in the way of his dreams.

"It would be a pleasure." Natalie smiled. "Come with me."

Nathan felt as if he were drunk, though he'd had nothing but mineral water for the last two hours.

"You're certain you can have that proposal ready by Thursday?" Stanley Allbright was long and lean with a hungry look. He was younger than Nathan expected for the Chief Financial Officer of a multinational corporation, but what he lacked in years he more than made up for in savvy. His questions had been blunt and to the point, and Nathan's mind had stretched and flexed to keep up.

"Not a problem." It would mean sleepless nights and cancelling a couple other meetings, but with Stanley's backing there was no way Mount Morgan could turn him down.

Julius Thames was less enthused and had been all along. His expression sour, he said, "I wish I'd been in on your first meeting."

Nathan could do nothing about internal politics, so simply nodded. "It certainly would have been helpful to have you with us." If Thames had been his boss, he, too, would have avoided having him peering over his shoulder whenever possible.

After Natalie had offered up introductions, Helen had adroitly drawn her and the political couple off to the side, leaving Nathan free to chat with the Mount Morgan execs. He had had no intention of monopolizing them for the whole evening, but Stanley hadn't let him escape.

Not that he wanted to. This was exactly what he'd needed—access to the top level of decision makers. But if he was honest, he had been jealous that the others were able to spend time with Helen, laughing and joking, without the pressure of having to perform.

The party was breaking up now, and Helen returned to his side. Without conscious thought he took her hand and squeezed it. How was he ever going to thank her for what she'd done?

He had one idea. But that was a discussion best left until they were home.

Helen had been thrilled to reconnect with Natalie. She considered the young woman a friend and would have been glad to catch up even if she hadn't been able to help Nathan with his aspirations. From his concentrated look and thoughtful silence as they drove home, she assumed things had gone well.

She was happy for him. She *was*. She could be happy and sad at the same time, couldn't she?

As she pondered the fact Nathan might be leaving Prince George, leaving *her*, a thought struck. Was it possible she was looking at everything from the wrong angle? What if her potential cancer and his probable promotion weren't obstacles to being lovers. What if they were what made it possible? They were no-harm-no-foul reasons either of them could escape from the relationship without messy recriminations.

A tiny voice warned getting closer to Nathan would inevitably lead to painful emotions, that she was naïve to think she could spend the next weeks making love with Nathan and *not* be hurt when it ended.

She ignored it and began planning how to present her proposal.

He pulled to a smooth stop inside his garage, leaving the wide door open behind them and Helen screwed up her courage. "I have a question."

"You do?" He blinked, as if coming back from deep thoughts. "I have something to ask you, too. Why don't you drop off your clubs at home and come back?"

"Okay." Her stomach twisted and turned. Did he intend to ask her the same thing? Were they finally on the same page? She hoped so.

He helped her remove her clubs from the back of his vehicle and she thanked him with a nod. After stowing them in her own garage, she headed to her en suite, stripped off her sweaty golf clothes and gave herself a quick sponge bath. Refreshed, she pondered what to wear. The maxi-dress she'd had on earlier didn't allow for a bra.

Nerves tingling, she slipped it on and headed to Nathan's.

The heat of the day was still trapped in the narrow space between his house and the fence. She reached through the black iron gate and lifted the latch, and then made her way to the back yard. Nathan was already on his patio, standing on the edge as was his habit, staring out over the lawn.

She hesitated in the shadows at the corner of the house and studied him. A thrum of desire rippled through her. She'd gripped those buttocks as he'd thrust inside her, bit the taut line of his neck, pressed her breasts against his broad chest.

And she wanted to do it again.

He rubbed his nape, his shirt riding up to reveal a line of skin at his waist. He had also changed and now wore a pale blue tee and khaki shorts. The muscles in his calves were smooth and strong. She swallowed and took a step forward.

"Hey." She paused where the grassy path met the patio.

He turned toward her, his pale blue gaze searing her as if he could see into her thoughts. "Hey."

Could she do this? Could she tell Nathan she wanted to have an affair with him for the short time they had remaining? He said something she didn't hear through the blood rushing loudly in her ears. "Sorry, what was that?"

"Want a drink?"

"Water would be great." She'd only had two glasses of wine at the tournament, but she felt tipsy and giddy. Maybe that was why she'd become mesmerized by his legs. Legs she'd seen a million times over the years.

He nodded and slid the glass door open. She knew the layout of his house like she knew her own, and she pictured him heading to the pale oak kitchen, getting a tumbler from the cupboard beside the fridge, and filling it from the tap. The scent of fresh cut grass surrounded her and the sound of children shouting drifted from the playground two streets over. She took a seat at the table, the mesh vinyl of the high-backed chair warm and pliant.

Nathan returned with two glasses, placed one in front of her and took a seat opposite. She sipped the cool liquid, ice cubes clinking, and then carefully placed it back in the circle of moisture it had left on the clear surface.

Maybe she should be a bit more subtle than the last time she'd asked him for sex. They might only have a few weeks together and she didn't want to waste any more time wallowing in misunderstandings and confusion.

"So where are we?" She watched a bead of liquid roll down the pale green glass. "Or rather, where do we go from here?"

He huffed out an amused breath. "We're in brand new territory. All I know for sure is I don't want to lose our friendship."

Relief was a cool wash through her veins. At least she would have that much. "Me, neither. I've done some thinking over the last few days." *And the last few minutes.* Not that she was willing to confess that. "We need to start fresh, from a point of honesty and clarity."

"If you mean forget we had sex, I don't think I can do that."

Her first thought was a panicked certainty he couldn't forgive her impulsive seduction. Then she saw the heat in his direct gaze and warmth flooded her belly.

"I don't want to forget it," he said bluntly, "because it was outstanding, and I want to do it again. But I definitely want to forgo unnecessary drama after."

Her fingers unclenched their grip on her glass. "Okay then. My question stands. Where do we go from here?"

Chapter Ten

Nathan twisted in his seat and lay one arm across the back. "Before we get to that, I want to thank you. For asking Natalie to introduce me to Allbright and Thames."

Caught up in her burgeoning lust, Helen paused a moment so she could reply calmly. "You're welcome. It was the least I could do. I take it your chat went well?"

"Very well. I am even more confident I'll close the sale now, and that puts the promotion very much in my reach."

"Good for you." She licked her lips, knowing she should be more effusive but not able to garner the necessary excitement. If Nathan was leaving for new adventures, she wanted her own adventures to start soon. Preferably now.

"It looks like I'm going to get what I want." He cocked his head and peered at her. "What about you? What do *you* want, Helen?"

I want you. She didn't think that was what he was talking about, though. "I might have cancer, remember?" The words were bitter on her tongue, but it didn't do to let him forget what might be in her future. "That makes it hard to make long-term plans. For now, I'm happy taking it one day at a time." That attitude is what had led them to this point, after all. If she could get him to think the same, the next few weeks could be a celebration, not a wake.

He wasn't to be deterred. "Forget cancer for now. If that weren't an issue...what would you want?"

She sighed. If she wanted to get him into bed anytime soon, she'd have to give in. "Sven has offered me Golden Dragon."

Nathan's eyes widened. "He has? Why?"

She explained the situation, and the longer she talked the brighter his expression grew. "That's awesome," he said when she finished. "You're going to do it, right?"

"I want to. But how can I commit to such a huge undertaking as things stand? I know you said forget cancer, but that would be irresponsible." *And impossible.*

"You're a smart woman. I'm sure you can figure something out, even if you get bad news." He took her hand in both of his and massaged her knuckles. "Now, let's get back to the main issue. What comes next for us."

"That is the reason I am here." She held back a purr as his fingers worked her joints. It was almost as good as a foot rub. "As I see it, we agree on the two most important points—we want to stay friends, and we want to have sex again. With each other."

He snorted a laugh. "Thanks for the clarification. But yes."

"Can we also agree that, just because we are having sex, there are no expectations that this is anything more than friends with benefits? And that either of us can end it at any time without explanations or excuses?" She had to make it clear she wouldn't hold it against him if he stepped back if she did have cancer but couldn't bear to put it directly into words.

He paused briefly in his ministrations before resuming with gentle force. "Agreed." Without releasing his grip on her hand, he leaned on the table, bringing their faces close together. The blue of his irises was almost transparent, the lashes surrounding them a golden brown. "Want to come to my bed now, Helen?"

Her heart fluttered making her breathless. "I do, Nathan. I really do."

Nathan knew Helen's invitation had been initiated by impulse.

His had been a deliberate declaration of desire.

He still wasn't sure if this was the right thing to do. But it felt like the *natural* thing to do. Helen was woven into the fabric of his life, and unravelling her would be painful, probably impossible.

He wanted to put off doing that as long as he could.

Her fingers trembled in his clasp as he led her into the house and up the stairs. She would know this was different than their first time together. By her own admission, she'd intended sex with him to be a one-time event.

Admitting she still wanted him moved them to an entirely different level.

Unlike Helen, Nathan had made no changes to the master bedroom he and Wanda had shared. Mostly because he no longer used it. Even before she'd become ill, he'd been sleeping in the spare room more often than not. When she died, he had no urge to move back into the room they'd shared in happier times. He halted at the foot of his bed and drew Helen toward him. She looked up, eyes wide and wondering. Her cap of greying hair hugged her skull, and he combed his fingers gently through the strands.

"Have I ever told you how much I like this look on you?" He cupped one hand around the nape of her neck, the soft, whiskery strands tickling his palm. "You have the most elegant skull."

Helen's laugh was soft and breathy. "That's the first time I've ever been told that."

"It's true." He laid his other hand flat on her breastbone, the vee between his thumb and forefinger framing the hollow at the base of her throat. Her heart thumped under his palm, the rhythm speeding up when he licked the corner of her mouth.

Her hands gripped his hips, and she arched her back, pressing her core against his growing erection. The thin, slippery fabric of her long dress slithered around his bare calves and his arms slid around her waist, sweeping her in tight.

While he held her, it was easy to let everything else go. He lost himself in her taste and scent, her warmth and softness. He trailed his fingers up the bumps of her spine, and she shuddered, pressing even closer. Her arms wound around his neck, embracing his head, her mouth open and her tongue demanding. Helen did nothing by halves, and to have her full attention made his knees weak.

He lowered himself to the bed. Helen remained standing, bending forward to keep their mouths melded together. In this position, the neckline of her dress gaped and he caught a glimpse of her breasts, unbound by a bra. His hands moved without thought, cupping the soft heaviness, and Helen's breath gasped into his mouth.

Remembering her responses from their first time together, he traced her nipples with his thumbs and they immediately rose into points. Helen moaned and let her weight press into his hold, her forearms resting on his shoulders, her hips undulating.

He leaned back and she followed, dragging her skirt out of the way, and crawling onto the mattress so that she ended up kneeling over his supine form. She didn't take her lips from his, her kisses growing short and frantic, mirroring her panting breath. He tweaked her nipples and her body froze for an instant, and then resumed its urgent movements. He pinched one and then the other, alternating the pressure from light to hard.

Gripping his wrists, keeping them in place, she sat upright, her weight settling on his groin. "Yes. Harder. More."

He followed her commands, watching through slitted lids as the flush on her cheeks seeped down her neck to her chest. His hips lifted in rhythm to his manipulation of her breasts, and she rubbed herself against his cock, trapped inside his shorts.

Her thighs tightened and she dropped forward, her hands clamping on his shoulders. Her fingers pinched as she threw her head back. A rush of damp heat soaked his groin. At the evidence of her orgasm, he almost came himself. Her hands slid down his ribs to his abdomen as she continued rocking. More heat, more wetness, and he couldn't hold back. Didn't want to hold back.

Sparkling explosions raced down his spine, gathered in his balls, up his cock. Jackknifing upright, he clutched Helen as his own orgasm burst, before dragging her down with him as he collapsed back against the mattress.

Helen tucked her head into the curve of Nathan's shoulder and tried to get her breath back. The sex had been even more amazing the second time around, and they hadn't even taken all their clothes off. He read her so well—knew instinctively how to wring out her deepest response. She could still feel his touch on her breasts, the way he'd played her into a frenzy until she could do nothing but fly off into oblivion.

What would sex be like without breasts? Hers had

always been so sensitive, so responsive. Despite the buzzing glow still shimmering in every cell of her body, she suddenly felt bereft, grief-stricken, and cursed her unpredictable emotions, so close to the surface these days. Her shoulders shuddered as she tried to control the welling tears. She was certain the last thing Nathan wanted to deal with after earthshaking sex was a bawling woman.

"Helen?" He shifted so they were nose to nose. She kept her eyes closed, ashamed to be making such a fuss. "Are you crying? Did I hurt you?"

She shook her head. "No. Of course not. I'm just being silly." Her words stuttered out on jagged breaths, shattering her attempt at rational speech.

"Tell me you're not regretting what we did already."

"No!" She opened her eyes and saw worry and concern in his. "Not at all. It was beautiful." Her throat burned.

"As long as you're sure." He searched her face.

"I'm sure. I promise." She put as much confidence as she could into her tone, hampered by her ballooning emotions. "Today's been a bit of a rollercoaster."

"Come here." Nathan rolled to his side and gathered her in. She draped one leg over his hip and snuggled in tight. His tenderness fractured the dam holding back her tears and she let them flow.

With her cheek on his chest, she felt rather than heard the words Nathan murmured. It really didn't matter what he was saying. His embrace was comfort and sanity and grace, and as her tears soaked his shirt she slowly relaxed, the wave of terror easing. As her breathing evened out and her sobs softened, Nathan's hold loosened, but he didn't release her until she raised herself on one elbow.

Swiping her wrist inelegantly under her streaming nose, she risked a glance at his face. He regarded her steadily, concern wrinkling his brow, simple acceptance in his eyes. "Sorry about that."

"You can cry on my shoulder anytime." He cupped her cheek and swept the pad of his thumb under her eye. "Want to talk about it?"

Uncertain, she dropped her gaze, and noted the large damp patch on his shirt. And the even larger one on the crotch of his shorts. Heat bloomed in a rushing remembrance of her abandon as she'd straddled his straining cock. "Maybe we should clean up." It gave her the perfect excuse to ignore his question.

Humour lightened the frown creasing his forehead. "How about I run a bath? Would you share it with me?"

They hadn't fully undressed to have sex. Now he was proposing they get naked in a tub. It sounded perfect. "I would. Thank you."

A few minutes later she leaned back against his chest, playing idly with the bubbles foaming around them. The large tub filled the corner of the master bedroom's en suite, with a window set high enough in the wall to provide privacy but allow the golden evening light to stream in.

Nathan's arms stretched along the edges of the tub, the skin darkening from his biceps to his hands in a soft-edged farmer's tan. His breath tickled the back of her neck. "So. Any particular reason for your tears? Is there something I should know?"

While she'd hoped he wouldn't return to the subject, she was grateful he'd avoided adding *else* to his latter question, given the revelations she made after their first time together. For an instant she considered prevaricating, but their truce was fragile and any lie, even by omission, could splinter it beyond repair. "I was thinking about sex without my breasts. Did you and Wanda—" She broke off, horrified by what she'd almost asked. "I'm sorry. That was much too personal."

He shifted, water sloshing, lifting his knees and cradling her between them. After a long pause, he said cautiously, "I know you and Wanda were good friends. Did she talk to you much about our marriage?"

"No." Helen felt a twinge of guilt, though it wasn't a lie. Wanda hadn't confided in Helen, but she would have had to be blind not to have seen the signs that all was not well between her friends.

"Our marriage was already in deep trouble before Wanda was diagnosed." Nathan's voice held complicated regret, and Helen took one of his hands and held it against her belly under the bubbles in a silent show of comfort. "I had decided to ask for a divorce, but then she told me about the cancer. I still loved her in a passive way, because of what we'd shared in the past, not because of what I could see in the future, and I couldn't abandon her. We tried to put things back together, but it was for all the wrong reasons. Sex hadn't been great before her mastectomy, and after, though we were intimate a few times, it wasn't a success. But I am sure it was a symptom of our relationship, not the surgery."

Helen let that sink in as she listened to the bubbles popping and fizzing. A strong relationship could weather a lot, she knew that. Despite their long history, though, her connection with Nathan felt thin and fragile.

Was it possible it could survive the next few weeks without imploding?

Chapter Eleven

The wire sticking out of her right breast was alien and intrusive. Helen couldn't look away from it, sickly fascinated, her thoughts cloudy from the light sedative pumping through the IV attached to her forearm.

"This will guide us directly to the mass," Dr. Chesley explained as the wire was inserted. "The surgeon will then remove the suspicious lump, as well as the surrounding tissue. Once we're done, we'll have you stay a little while longer to make sure you're feeling okay, but you'll be free to go home soon after. Do you have someone coming to pick you up?"

Helen nodded, her head wobbly on her neck. "A friend. He's waiting for me to text him."

"Great." Dr. Chesley patted her knee. "Okay, let's get you to the surgeon."

Helen walked to the room where the biopsy was to take place in a foggy haze, everything out of focus and soft-edged. Her breast was frozen with local anesthetic and the procedure wasn't painful, though she could feel tugging and pressure. She'd been arranged in such a way she couldn't watch what was going on, even if she'd wanted to.

She allowed herself to float, her hazy thoughts drifting over the last couple of days. After sharing the bath with Nathan on Sunday evening, Helen had headed home with relief. The solitude of her own space was welcome after the intensity of recent emotions, and she'd fallen into bed early, sleeping solidly through the night.

She waited until Nathan had left for work before leaving to cover her shift at Golden Dragon. It was cowardly, but after her meltdown she needed a little longer before facing him. While he'd been nothing but supportive, comforting a weeping woman was more than a sex buddy should be expected to endure.

By that evening, however, the urge to be with him was stronger than any awkwardness, so a few minutes after his normal arrival time she sent him a text.

Come for dinner? Hamburgers on the grill.

She waited several nail-biting minutes—long enough to begin second-guessing her invitation—before the three dots next to Nathan's name blinked into life.

Working late tonight. Won't be home until after eight.

She stared at the screen, brow furrowed. What did that mean? He hadn't said no, but it wasn't a yes, either. She nibbled her lip, and then figured she might as well go all in. *That's fine, I can wait.*

His reply to that had been instantaneous. *I'll bring the wine.*

It was closer to nine by the time he climbed the stairs to the back deck where Helen reclined on the outdoor sofa. Her anxiety level had ratcheted back up, causing her to check her phone compulsively for a cancellation text. Unable to speak from relief, she sent him a cool, casual smile while her pulse trip hammered in her throat.

"I'm so sorry. I'm slammed putting the Mount Morgan proposal together." He bent to kiss her cheek and then straightened, offering the bottle of malbec he carried. "I brought your favourite. Forgive me?"

"There's nothing to forgive." She rose to her feet and found herself nose to chin with Nathan. His gaze sharpened and she imagined him shaking off the last of his work worries. "I assume you want a glass, too?"

"Definitely. Do you need help getting dinner ready, or would you like me to fire up the grill?"

"Grill, please. I'm starving."

"I really am sorry. I should have said I couldn't make it."

His brow creased and she gave into the impulse to smooth it with her fingertips. "It's fine, honestly. I understand how important this project is for you. And I'm a big girl. If I wanted to eat sooner, I would have."

He clasped her hand and brought her fingers to his mouth, sucking gently on the tips. "I'll make it up to you." The low timbre of his voice rolled up her arm directly to her belly.

"And I'll let you." Breathless and dizzy, she stepped away. If she let him touch her more, dinner would be even later. "But first, let's eat."

Afterward, they settled on the outdoor sofa and it felt entirely natural for Helen to curl her legs up and lay her head on his shoulder.

"Feeling better?" he asked, his arm encircling her, his fingertips tracing a featherlight pattern on her bicep.

"I'm stuffed. I shouldn't have had that extra helping of potato salad."

"I'm not talking about dinner."

"Oh." She'd wondered if he would mention her freak out and wasn't sure how to feel now that he had. "I am. Thank you for asking."

"No problem. That's what friends are for." His sigh whistled out, riffling the short strands of hair on the top of her head. "Don't be afraid to ask me for help, Helen. Anything you need." He kissed the crown of her head.

Ask me for help. If only it were that simple.

Then Helen remembered it *was* that simple. She could ask Nathan for help because he was already leaving, so she didn't have to worry that it was her neediness that had shoved him away.

Still, it took a concerted effort to make her lips and tongue form the words she needed to say. "There is something you could do for me." She kept her head on his shoulder so she couldn't see his face. This was hard enough without making eye contact. "I'm not allowed to drive myself home after the biopsy. I could always take a taxi, but—"

He didn't let her finish. "Just tell me when and where."

"I have to be at the hospital by eight on Wednesday. I don't know how long I'll be, so I'd have to text you."

He didn't speak for a moment, and then his shoulder raised and lowered, joggling her lightly. "Consider it a date."

Helen blinked sleepily as Dr. Chesley came into her field of view.

"All done."

She struggled to pull her into focus, disoriented from the sedative and her wandering thoughts. "Really?"

"Really really." The other woman smiled, her mouth hidden by her mask but her eyes crinkling. "We'll get you into recovery in a minute and you should be good to go soon."

"How does it look? Did you get everything?"

With typical medical reticence, Dr. Chesley gave a noncommittal answer. "We'll know more once the pathologist has a look. Until then, you need to rest and recover. Be a patient patient."

Helen giggled. "I only think that's funny because of the drugs."

"The waiting can be difficult. Find something to occupy your mind, or it will feel like forever."

Helen didn't think *anything* would fit that bill, but she nodded agreeably. Despite the trouble it had caused, she was glad Nathan knew what was going on. At least she had someone to talk to, to share her anxieties with.

She'd better not get used to it. He wouldn't be around forever, not with the promotion looming in his future. For now, though, she'd take what she could get.

Nathan forced his concentration back to the print copy of his Mount Morgan proposal. He was going over it for the fifth time, and he still kept finding things he wanted to change. He didn't care. He was determined it would be perfect. It had to be.

His eyes were drawn once more to the clock in the corner of his computer screen. Helen hadn't texted yet, and he was beginning to worry something had gone awry.

Who was he kidding? He'd been worried all day.

Helen had been determinedly cheerful this morning on their way to the hospital, and he'd done his best to match her positive energy. He'd offered to go in with her and wasn't sure whether he was relieved or disappointed when she'd politely but firmly rejected the idea.

"This is no big deal," she'd said, pecking him on the cheek as she opened her door. "A simple, quick procedure. You've got more important things to do than waste your time lurking in the waiting room. I'll text when I'm ready to be picked up. Go, get prepped for tomorrow. It's going to be the sale of your life."

He'd smiled, as she'd intended, but it had slipped off his face the moment she was out of sight. At the office, he'd holed up to put the last touches on the proposal, but despite knowing it was the most important one he'd ever worked on, he'd had a difficult time focusing. His thoughts had been perpetually drawn to what Helen was going through at any given moment. He had a good idea of what the procedure entailed, and while it didn't sound pleasant, he knew it was much less invasive than any future treatments might be.

As he well knew from Wanda's experience.

With a twinge of guilt, he couldn't help comparing Helen's fierce independence with Wanda's terrified vulnerability. She had clung to him with all her might, physically and emotionally, and while he couldn't blame her, it had exhausted him, wrung him out. Not that he'd ever complained about her neediness, to her or anyone else. He wasn't that much of a jerk. But while the embers of his resentment had been doused, they still flared up at unexpected moments.

Like now.

He shifted in his seat, tossing down the thick sheaf of pages he'd been perusing and rubbing his temples. He didn't resent Helen. He *didn't*. She hadn't asked him to give anything more than he'd offered. She had sent him to work, telling him to concentrate on his career and not worry about her.

As if that were even possible. If he were honest, he was a basket case. And this was the easy part. What if the tumour wasn't the benign cyst she insisted it was? Could he accept the promotion and the move to the Island it demanded if Helen were wrong?

The idea of abandoning her was a black cloud tainting what should have been one of the most exciting times in his professional career. He shuddered at the word his subconscious had dredged up. *Abandon*. Is that really what his inner self thought he'd be doing if he accepted the promotion should it be offered?

His phone alerted to a text. Relieved to put aside his discombobulating thoughts, he snatched it up from the desk. Helen. *I'm ready. Meet you at the main doors.*

She had been adamant she just needed the ride, that once she was home she'd be fine on her own and he could return to work. He scanned his mental To Do list—much of which still needed to be done, given the little he'd accomplished. But even as he did so, he picked up his desk phone to call Melanie. She answered after one ring.

"Hey," he said. "I'm heading out for the rest of the day."

"Everything okay?" She sounded concerned, but not disapproving. "Is the proposal done?"

"Everything's fine. A friend needs my help. I have a couple more tweaks, but I'll work on them at home. I'll email you the final version as soon as I can." As his supervisor, Melanie had a vested interest in seeing him make the sale and had also been a great sounding board for his ideas.

"Okay," she said. "See you tomorrow."

He heard the faint question in her tone and answered firmly. "You bet. Wild horses couldn't keep me away." As he disconnected, he admitted he'd miss working for Melanie. She was a very hands-off manager, trusting her staff to do their jobs, letting the numbers do the talking. Moving up the ladder didn't mean he wouldn't have a boss to answer to. Now he came to think of it, Melanie had occasionally ranted uncomplimentary things about the man Nathan would be responsible to should he get the new position.

He texted Helen to tell her he was on his way, his shoulders lighter than they had been in days. He was doing the right thing, putting work on the back burner to take care of his friend. *My lover*, he corrected himself.

It felt more than right. It felt like the only thing he could do.

Chapter Twelve

The evening after the biopsy, Helen's breast was swollen and bruised, yet if she were careful and moved deliberately, she could do everything she needed to without real pain. Not that she needed to do much at all, as Nathan barely left her side. That hadn't been the plan—she'd intended he simply drive her home and then get back to work—but he'd surprised and touched her by announcing he'd made other arrangements and wasn't going anywhere.

The sedative had left her feeling woozy and for the first few hours all she did was lay on the couch, watch the Food Network and drift. Nathan was quietly attentive, refreshing the ice packs she used to minimize the swelling at the surgical site and brewing multiple cups of tea, which she accepted, and offering crackers and fruit, which she declined. When she did grow hungry, he made her chicken soup as if she were suffering from a fever, and whether it was his ministrations or simply the passage of time, by ten o'clock she was feeling back to normal. So normal she became vaguely irritated at his hovering and shooed him home.

"Thanks for everything," she said, every syllable sincere. "I'll be fine on my own for the night." Which was also the truth. She needed to be alone, needed to stop putting on a brave face for at least a few hours.

"Of course you will." He gathered the dishes that cluttered the coffee table and brought them to the kitchen, and then returned to loom over her with a worried expression. "Are you sure? I can stay if you want."

She raised herself to her feet, moving gingerly, testing herself. "I'm sure. Besides, you need to get some rest before your big presentation tomorrow. You won't do that if you're here, pandering to my every wish."

He smiled at her hyperbole and then moved toward the front door. Helen stepped down the short flight of stairs gingerly, relieved her limbs once again felt connected to her body. "I appreciate everything you've done today. I know it was bad timing for you, with Mount Morgan and everything."

"I would never not make time for you, Helen." His hand on the doorknob, he hesitated. "About tomorrow. I don't feel right leaving you on your own all day."

"Are you offering to cancel your meeting?" She said it jokingly, so was surprised by the hurt that stabbed her chest when his eyes widened to show the whites around his irises. Irritation at her weakness caused her to speak more sharply than maybe she should have. "I didn't mean it, Nathan. Don't look so horrified."

His expression flattened too late to hide his true reaction. "I would if I could but—"

"I said I didn't mean it. I'll be fine on my own." *This* was why she didn't ask for help. It made people feel pressured and guilty.

"Maybe Megan could—"

"*No.*" She cut him off a second time. "No. Megan couldn't, because Megan doesn't know about this. She *can't* know about this." Helen gripped his wrist and shook it for emphasis. "When I tell her or anyone else is my call, my decision, not yours. You promised you wouldn't say anything about the biopsy."

"I did, but I don't feel right—"

She interrupted him a third time, fighting off full-scale panic. "No one can know, Nathan. I mean it. Promise me again."

The depth of her fear finally got through to him. His look of exasperation faded. "I won't tell anyone about the biopsy, or the reason for it. I promise."

She searched his face and saw nothing but sincerity and concern. Her death grip on his arm eased. "Please, don't make me regret telling you."

"I won't." His hand cupped her cheek, and he kissed her gently on the forehead as if to seal his vow.

A flutter of emotion wriggled in her belly and, for a second, she sagged against him. "Thank you. Goodnight, Nathan."

"Goodnight, Helen." He stepped through the door, and she closed it behind him. Through the frosted glass window, she could see the gleam of the outdoor light glowing down on his vague form, and then he was gone.

Soon, he'd be gone for good. It was time to start getting used to the idea.

She dragged herself up the stairs and down the hall. Without bothering to brush her teeth, she curled up in bed and let the dregs of the drugs lull her into a restless sleep.

When Nathan strode into the Mount Morgan Mining boardroom Thursday morning, he was surprised to see Stanley Allbright and Julius Thames seated with the Specialist in Vendor Management and other team members he'd met the week before.

After the obligatory round of handshakes, he nodded at the two men. "Stanley. Julius. I didn't expect to see you here today." He smiled to take any perception of criticism from the words. Advanced notice of their presence wouldn't have changed his presentation, though it did make his adrenaline pump faster now.

"We always intended to spend a week in Prince George." Julius spoke as if Nathan should have known that fact, his expression as disapproving as it had been at the golf tournament.

"I assume you don't mind." Stanley's tone, while friendly, brooked no disagreement.

"Of course not. I'm flattered you decided to attend. I am sure you're very busy." He slid his laptop out of its case and hooked it up to the monitor attached to a wheeled stand at the end of the table. "Shall we begin?"

Nathan had thought the time he'd spent with the Mount Morgan executives on Sunday had been intense. By the time the meeting was over, he realized he'd only seen them in their laidback, casual roles. Stanley and Julius zeroed in on every potential issue, every possible crack in the contract, and he'd been kept hopping to answer their insightful questions. He was glad he'd put so much effort into his proposal because their analysis left nothing unturned.

Finally, they'd wrung every last drop they could out of the discussion and the meeting began to break up. The Specialist of Vendor Management gave Nathan a sympathetic nod, as if she knew how demanding the last two hours had been, and he returned it with a grin from which he tried to hide his elation. His blood was racing with excitement. He'd done well, he knew it. His instincts were telling him the deal was as good as signed.

Julius escorted Nathan to the front door. While his expression was still severe, the courteous gesture sent Nathan's hopes soaring even higher. "Nice presentation." Julius held out his hand and Nathan shook it. "We'll be in touch within the week."

The inside of Nathan's vehicle was hot and stifling. He turned the air conditioning to its max and let the cool air wash over him.

His longed-for promotion was in his grasp. He couldn't wait to tell Helen. She'd be thrilled for him. He pictured her wide grin, her green eyes alight with joy at his success. The rush of warmth was immediately followed by a chill that rivalled the icy air blasting from the vents.

Achieving his dream meant leaving Prince George and all he'd built there. Leaving Helen.

He hadn't allowed himself to think of her until now. Of course, he had, because such a goal was impossible. But he had managed to keep her at the back of his mind.

He'd found a special sort of comfort in caring for her yesterday. While he'd had to fit in working on the final pieces of his proposal between offering her food and drink and pain relievers, he'd felt balanced, as if both parts of his life complemented, not diminished, the other. And when she'd sent him on his way, he hadn't wanted to go, even though he knew she was right. He couldn't encourage her to lean on him, not when he wouldn't be around for long.

As he put the car in gear and headed back to his office to tell Melanie the hopeful news, he pondered what he should do about Helen. If he knew she had people to rely on once he was gone, maybe his nagging sense of guilt would ease.

He'd promised he wouldn't tell anyone about the biopsy. But that didn't mean he couldn't call in a few favours, did it?

Without work to distract her during the two days after her surgery, Helen grew fractious and cranky. On

Friday evening, she was sulking on the back deck when Nathan carried a flat box down the path between their houses and up the stairs.

"How are you feeling?" He placed the container on the low table in front of her. The savoury richness of cheese and pepperoni and tomato sauce wafted toward her, and she scowled.

"Stop asking me. I'm fine. Bored out of my mind, but fine." It wasn't fair to take out her frustrations on him, but it was his own fault for being handy. He'd brought her dinner the night before, too, but the novelty of being taken care of had worn paper thin. Pushing aside her unreasonable grumpiness, she said, "How was work? Any news from Mount Morgan?"

Nathan had been uncharacteristically quiet about yesterday's meeting. He'd told her it had gone well, but given no specifics, as if he didn't want to jinx it.

Which meant he believed he had an excellent chance at closing the deal.

Which gave her the selfish urge to yell *shutout* in a superstitious attempt to derail his dream.

Which made her a terrible friend.

"Not yet, but I wasn't expecting anything today." He gestured with his thumb toward the house. "I'll get the plates."

He had no way of knowing about her inner turmoil—which illogically made her angrier yet. "No. I will," she snapped. It was time he stopped treating her as if she were helpless. She shifted to stand and winced when she used her right arm for leverage.

Nathan was at her side instantly, his hand on her elbow. "Are you okay?"

"How many times do I have to tell you I'm fine?" She shrugged off his light grip. The twinges were nothing she couldn't handle, would be little more than a nuisance if they didn't constantly remind her she was waiting for results that would determine her future. Or lack of it.

He studied her with narrowed eyes and then dropped onto a seat, stretching his legs out. "I'll wait here, then."

It was easy enough to dig out the napkins and silverware, and if she had to take the plates down from an upper cupboard with her left hand that was no big deal. She placed everything neatly on a large bamboo serving tray, added two wine glasses and an unopened bottle of pinot grigio, and gripped the handles.

The ache in her right breast intensified with the strain but she gritted her teeth and headed outside.

Nathan shot to his feet. "Damn it, Helen! You're not supposed to carry anything more than five pounds."

"And I'm not." She had no idea how much it all weighed, of course, but only the wine bottle had any heft to it. He snatched it away and she felt immediate relief which she refused to show. Bending over to place the tray on the table beside the pizza box had the breath hissing from her tightly clenched jaw and she couldn't hold back a sigh once it was safely lowered.

"I knew you were stubborn," Nathan said, "but I had no idea *how* stubborn."

"I am not an invalid. I had minor surgery that is already healing. If you're going to act like this, you can take your pizza and go home." She seated herself and surreptitiously cradled her right elbow in her left hand. "I won't get the results back for more than a week. I have to keep busy, or I'll go crazy."

Dr. Chesley had warned her the delay might be longer than usual as the surgery had been done before a long weekend. The first Monday in August was a statutory holiday in British Columbia, and often the hottest weekend of the year, even when they weren't in the middle of a heat wave. Normally she would spend it with Megan, her dentist husband Nicholas, and Nora, but she'd begged off the usual family events not sure she'd be up to taking part and unwilling to risk extended time under Megan's eagle eyes.

"You won't do yourself any good if you screw up your recovery." Nathan slid a piece of pizza onto a plate and handed it to Helen.

She took it without thanks. "That's the last thing I want to do. But I can't sit here and do nothing." She wasn't shifted to be back at Golden Dragon for almost a week. If she'd been able to plan for the takeover, she'd have something to occupy her mind, but she couldn't make any decisions until the results were in. It was a vicious circle.

One she was sick and tired of travelling.

Chapter Thirteen

The thick but fluffy crust was hot on her fingers. Helen glared at the slice, annoyed with herself, it, and the whole world. Nathan regarded her with his head tilted to one side and a compassionate expression, and she added him to her list of annoyances.

"Why don't we go out tonight?" Nathan blew on the slice propped on his fingertips. "There's a jazz duo playing at Café Voltaire."

She bit off the end of the triangle with a ferocious chomp. It was her favourite pizza from her favourite restaurant, but it glommed into a gluey, tasteless mass. She swallowed it down.

"I don't know anything about jazz." She paused, hearing the petulance in her voice. It was time to stop acting like a three-year-old. "But I'm willing to learn. Do you want to go?"

"I suggested it, didn't I? No alcohol, as you're on pain meds. And you need your rest so right home after." He scowled at her to emphasize his point. "But at least you'll be out of the house."

She chewed her pizza with growing enthusiasm. "I know it's only been a couple days, but I feel like I've been in jail. I can be ready in half an hour."

Nathan laughed. "I don't think we're in that much of a rush. Enjoy your meal, first."

Maybe it was pathetic to be so excited about an evening at a coffee shop. But it was an evening out with Nathan, and as they hadn't been out in public as a couple yet, it felt rather like a first date.

She started planning what to wear.

The first person she saw when they arrived at Café Voltaire was Terrance Renfrew. He stood at the order counter, a light scarf draped over his teal blue silk shirt, khakis neatly pressed, debonair as always despite the heat.

"Hello, there!" With her left arm, she gave him a careful hug, the short bristles of his goatee catching in her hair. "Fancy meeting you here!"

"It is?" He blinked, lashes fluttering over dark eyes.

"We didn't know we were coming until a little while ago." Nathan clapped the other man on the shoulder. "Is Bennett here?"

Terrance lifted his eyebrows. "Of course. Over there, with Penta and Stephanie."

"There are more of us here?" Helen peered around Terrance, searching the crowded tables.

"What a coincidence." Something in Nathan's tone niggled Helen's instincts, but he asked her what she wanted to drink and shooed her toward the table with the other Silverberries before she could catch it.

"Hi, Helen!" Penta Potter beamed as she approached, her cheeks round in her cheerful face. "Won't this be fun?"

The café was so small the jazz duo were only a few feet away, but the smooth, mellow tones of the saxophone and cool, crisp piano notes were subtle enough to allow for easy conversation. Helen took a seat. "It sounds great already. Do you come often?"

Penta flushed. Helen cursed herself. Penta was

recently separated from her husband and had four or five children—Helen should know by now but could never remember—and was sensitive to any insinuation she was failing as a mother.

"I only meant..."

Stephanie rescued her before she could make things worse. In her deep tones, she said, "Terrance and Bennett and I have been a few times. We enjoy it."

With relief Helen turned to the other woman. She had met Stephanie for the first time at the last book club meeting, but beyond her name didn't remember much about her. That evening was mostly a blur, except for everything that had happened with Nathan. *That* she remembered with spinetingling clarity. "I know very little about jazz, to be honest."

"I don't either, so I just sit back and listen." Stephanie was a touch overdressed in a midnight blue, slim-fitting sheath. An above averagely tall woman, she had excellently done makeup and blonde hair in a stylish cut that swung forward along her jawline.

Terrance and Nathan arrived with drinks all round, and in the flurry of activity Helen's tension eased.

Until Bennett said, "So, how are you feeling?" Terrance jerked and Bennett winced. "What was that for?"

Helen realized the former had kicked the latter, and the hints fell into place like dominoes. Terrance's confusion when she was surprised to see him, Nathan's hurry to get Helen to the table, Penta's overly cheerful greeting.

She had to be wrong. Nathan wouldn't betray her by telling the Silverberries about her biopsy. He *wouldn't*. Would he?

Clutching her composure tightly, she said to Bennett, "Why do you ask?"

"Uh, no reason. How are *you* doing, Penta?" Bennett was younger and taller than Terrance, with tightly curled dark hair and clean-cut features. Helen didn't know him as well as she knew Terrance, who had been a colleague of Aaron's. But she didn't need to know him well to recognize he was a man scrambling to cover up a mistake.

The muscles of her neck brittle with outrage, Helen turned her head and stared at Nathan, seated on her left. "You told them. How could you do that to me?"

The jazz duo crescendoed into a triumphant flurry of notes followed by a sudden silence, the ironic accompaniment to the shattering of Helen's trust.

The hurt and betrayal in Helen's eyes sucked the air from Nathan's lungs.

"No!" He should have known she'd jump to this conclusion. Once again, he'd underestimated her need for privacy. "I didn't tell them anything."

"Then why the guilty faces?" Without taking her concentration from him, she waved at hand at the group.

Seeking respite from her accusing glare, he scanned the table and saw expressions of confusion and dismay. No guilt though, no matter what Helen said. That was reserved for him. Because while he hadn't broken his promise, he had bent it badly out of shape. "All I told them was you were going through some health issues. had had a rough week and would enjoy time with friends."

Her eyes narrowed in suspicion. "I don't believe you."

Terrance entered the fray. "He's telling the truth, Helen. He didn't give us any details, and we don't want them. But we do want you to know you have us in your corner." Penta nodded vigorously and Stephanie gave a sharp jerk of her chin. Nathan held his breath.

"I didn't mean to pry." Bennett fidgeted with his silverware. "It was just a reflex. Honestly."

No one but Helen would have heard a threat in an innocent question. Nathan hadn't realized she was *that* rabid about her independence. What burdens had she carried alone before now? He'd done his best while Aaron was sick, but looking back he saw he was the one that initiated all the contact, not Helen. What else had she hidden from him?

"Helen." He laid his hand on hers where it lay fisted on the table. He took heart when she didn't pull away. "These people are your friends. They're not going to ask anything of you that you aren't prepared to give."

Her fingers loosened a fraction. "You really didn't say anything about..." She trailed off, her pinched features softening, giving her an air of wistful vulnerability that shredded his heart.

"Nothing. I give you my word."

"So they came because..."

Penta leaned in. "Because we like you and want to help. In any way you'll let us." She fixed Helen with a steady look. "We all need help sometimes."

Nathan allowed his attention to drift from Helen just long enough to wonder if maybe the Silverberries had failed Penta in her recent troubles. But that was a concern for another day.

Then it struck him. These people would be only fond memories once he began his new life on the Island. They weren't the type of friends he would keep in touch with. The thought filled him with soft sorrow.

Helen turned her hand over and gripped his, and the last of the stiffness in her spine eased away. "Well, thank you all. Even you." The sideways glance she slid Nathan held forgiveness. Not forgetfulness, but forgiveness. For now, he'd take that small gift.

As Helen and Nathan made their goodbyes to the Silverberries at the end of the evening, she admitted they had been a delightful distraction from the worries consuming her. But the laughter and conversation had been evidence of something deeper.

No matter how closely she watched them, she could find no signs they resented or begrudged Nathan's request. They had responded promptly and cheerfully to his summons and had then done their best to ensure she had a congenial evening. It was an enlightening discovery.

Maybe she didn't have to do this alone. Or not as alone as she'd planned, anyway.

Nathan walked her to her front step just after midnight. The cool, dark air swirled around them, a relief from the unrelenting high temperatures during the day.

"Have you heard when this heat wave is expected to break?" She fit her key in the lock and opened the door.

"Next week sometime."

Nathan's breath on the back of her neck made her shiver and she turned to face him. The beams from the porchlight overhead cast shadows on his face and for a moment he looked unfamiliar, mysterious. His collar was rolled underneath, and she straightened it before letting her palms rest on his chest. "Are you coming in?"

"I'm forgiven, then?" His hands came to her hips, his thumbs tracing small circles.

While she believed he hadn't given away all her secrets, he *had* bent her trust. She released the last pinch of betrayal. "Yes."

"All I wanted to do was show you that you have friends that will back you up."

"I know. Thank you. It was a wonderful evening."

"I'm glad you enjoyed it." His mouth brushed hers

softly, once, twice.

Liquid passion washed through her veins with a rising heat. She lifted on tiptoe to bring her centre in line with the hard ridge already forming at his groin. Her spine lined up with the edge of the doorframe and his weight pressed her against it while his lips and tongue danced with hers.

"I've missed this." His words were breathy and rough.

"Me, too." With sudden urgency she stretched her arms over his shoulders to grip his skull. A whistle of discomfort hissed from her lips as the movement tugged at the surgery site.

Nathan drew back immediately. "Did you hurt yourself?"

She shook her head. "No. Just a twinge." She lifted her chin, seeking his mouth again, but he tilted away.

"Maybe this isn't a good idea."

Determined to taste him, she nibbled along the tight tendon of his neck. "Oh, it's a good idea all right. We'll be careful."

"Let's wait one more night." He stepped back, keeping his hands on her hips to prevent her from following. "I have an idea. We'll go to my cabin tomorrow morning. Why waste all this wonderful weather in town? And if you're feeling good that evening..." He waggled his brows suggestively.

Helen laughed, despite her disappointment. "Fine. I had no idea you were such a worrier." But if he thought she'd wait until evening, he had another think coming. She'd let him deny her tonight, but she had no intention of waiting much past getting settled in the cabin. She'd almost ruined his thoughtful gesture by her initial ungrateful reaction. She owed him.

And she intended to pay up in creative and passionate ways.

Chapter Fourteen

As expected, the heat wave continued through the weekend. Their days at the cabin were hot, sunny, and relaxing. Helen chose to think about things other than test results, tattoo parlors, and temporary friends-with-benefits, choosing to live in the moment. And since those moments included paddling gently through cool crisp water, lounging sleepily in summer sunshine, and making tenderly passionate love, life was as good as it had been in years.

On the drive out Saturday morning, she'd wondered if it would feel odd spending so much time with Nathan with no one around to create a buffer. In the past that buffer had been family, and more recently it had been the members of the Silverberry Book Club. Instead, it felt right. So right, that when they pulled into Nathan's driveway on Monday evening, she didn't want to go back to her single, solitary existence.

Nathan, however, gave no indication he wanted to continue their nights together, and she had to respect the fact that he might need some time to himself. He'd been caring and thoughtful all weekend and she kissed him goodbye with gratitude, letting enough heat seep into it that his eyes were dazed when she pulled away. "See you later." She patted his cheek. "Thanks for everything."

"You are more than welcome." His fingers trailed up and down her bare arm. "See you tomorrow after work?"

"I've invited Nora to spend the night to make up for not seeing her last week. If you want to join us for tea parties and Legos, feel free to drop by for the evening." She didn't think it necessary to spell out an adult sleepover was off limits with Nora in the house. Especially since Nora would expect to be the one sharing Helen's bed, as she always did.

His mouth quirked in a half grin, and she knew he understood. "It's all good. I'll call you later."

She had trouble sleeping Monday and told herself it was just getting used to the noise of the city after the utter stillness at the cabin. Tuesday, she kept busy with housework she'd put off and laundry that needed doing, and by the time Megan brought Nora she was more than ready for the company.

After a swift hello hug, Nora raced up the stairs to put her backpack in Helen's bedroom.

"Don't I get a kiss goodbye?" Megan called after her.

"Just a minute, Mommy. I'll be right back."

Cool and casual in denim capris and a pale green T-shirt, Megan shook her head ruefully. "I'm chopped liver when you're around."

"Don't worry. It gets worse. Wait until she's a teenager."

Megan snorted. "How was your weekend? You look like you got some sun."

"I did." Helen shifted uncomfortably. As far as Megan knew, she'd spent the last few days in her back yard. Nathan's cabin had cell service, and Helen hadn't bothered to tell her daughter about her last-minute change in plans. She had no idea how Megan might react to knowing she and Nathan were...whatever they were. It was one more secret she had to keep.

Her daughter's gaze sharpened, and she leaned forward, peering at Helen's chest. "Is that a bruise?"

Helen glanced down, belatedly shielding the surgery area with her left hand. The pain from the biopsy had subsided, and she'd forgotten about the discolourations on the upper slope of her breast and into her armpit, revealed by the thin straps of her tank top. "This? It's nothing."

"It's an odd spot for a contusion."

"Uhm..." Helen scrambled for an answer that would pacify her doctor daughter—but not quickly enough.

"Did you have a biopsy?" Megan's voice rose in pitch. "Mom? What's going on?"

Before she could decide whether to tell the truth or stick with her denial, Nora pattered down the hall. "I'm ready now. I've unpacked and everything." Standing on the top of the short flight of stairs leading to the front door, she puckered her lips. "Kiss goodbye, Mommy."

Megan turned her head and stretched up to allow her daughter to kiss her cheek. "Goodnight, sweetie. See you tomorrow." Her gimlet gaze remained fastened on Helen. "I need to talk to Gramma for a minute longer. Why don't you go put on a movie and she'll be there soon?"

Nora scampered away, disappearing into the family room off the kitchen. Keeping her voice low, Megan said, "Enough, Mom. I want the truth."

"Fine." Helen squeezed her eyes shut, wishing it were possible to shut off reality that easily. Her racing pulse clogged her throat, and she swallowed down the memories of her twenty-year-old self. Her own mother had announced her diagnosis with a grim satisfaction, certain that Helen would now abandon university—a bid for freedom she had fought bitterly to prevent—and return home to succor to her every need.

Megan wasn't Helen, and Helen *definitely* wasn't her mother. If the Silverberry Book Club hadn't run screaming away, why would her own daughter?

Taking a deep breath she met Megan's stare. "Yes, I had a biopsy."

"And you were going to tell me when?" Megan's face paled, her tone flat and cold.

She hadn't expected her daughter to be *angry*. What did she have to be angry about? Helen had only been trying to shield her. "If the results came back positive for cancer."

Megan's expression hardened further. "You mean if they came back negative, you were going to act as if nothing had happened?"

"If they are negative, there will be nothing to tell." Still confused by Megan's reaction, she couldn't keep a note of pleading from her voice.

"Mom." Megan heaved an exasperated sigh and shook her head. "You don't have to handle everything on your own. I can help. I *want* to help."

Braced for rejection, the conversation wasn't going anything like Helen had feared. But Megan's offer was still unacceptable. "No. That's not necessary. I am perfectly capable of looking after myself." She would never allow Megan to put her own life on hold to care for an ailing mother. She might think she wanted to do so now, but she'd soon come to resent Helen.

"That's not the point. When Dad was sick..." Megan paused, drawing in a slow breath. "When Dad was sick, I had to practically beat the details out of you. Do you know how frightened and alone that made me feel?"

Helen stared at her, astonished. "We didn't want you to worry."

"Of course I worried! I could see Dad was dying. I was in my final years of med school. I'd seen enough cancer patients to recognize the signs. But every time

I tried to help, you pushed me away." Tears glistened, unshed, in the corner of her eyes.

"Oh, baby." Helen rushed forward and took Megan in her arms. Her daughter was taller than her, so it was impossible to gather her in, tuck her under her chin as Helen done when Megan was a child. "I'm so sorry. We didn't mean to make things worse."

"I won't do it again." Megan embraced her, bending her head so their cheeks brushed together. "I won't let you shut me out this time. No matter what. I love you too much."

"I love you, too." Helen sniffed to hold back her tears, gave Megan one last squeeze, and released her. "Ask me anything. I'll tell you whatever you want."

On familiar ground, Megan quizzed her and Helen answered honestly. Then Megan said, "You didn't drive home after the procedure, did you? How did you get back?"

The urge to hedge her answer was strong, but she'd promised Megan she'd tell the truth. "Nathan drove me." She did her best to sound as if that were no big deal.

Megan blinked. "Mr. Spieth?" Her cheeks flushed and Helen watched nervously for a return of her original anger. Instead, a speculative gleam sparked in her eyes. "You told our next-door neighbour about your biopsy and you didn't tell *me*?"

"Uhm..."

"Are you sleeping with Mr. Spieth?"

Why did Megan have to be so smart, so intuitive? The corners of Helen's mouth turn down in a sulky pout that made her feel like a teenager. "That's none of your business."

Megan stared at her, and then toed off her sandals. "All right. I'm not going anywhere until you tell me everything. No more secrets." She took Helen by the elbow and dragged her to the kitchen. "We're going to need wine."

Nathan was at his desk Wednesday morning, gathering his paraphernalia to head out of the office and spend another day not thinking about Mount Morgan and the looming deadline—or Helen and their growing connection. One or the other had dominated any unguarded moments since Monday evening, and his nerves were frayed and ragged.

When his cell phone rang, his first thought was *Helen.* He'd hoped spending the weekend with her might have soothed some of his hunger. It hadn't. Without her near enough to touch, he hadn't slept well Monday, and then Nora's visit had meant he'd stayed away Tuesday as well. Maybe this was a call inviting him over after work today.

It wasn't. The display on his screen read *Mount Morgan.*

The phone rang a second time before he had a chance to gather his composure. His pulse racing, he answered. "Nathan Spieth."

"Stanley Allbright here."

His sweaty grip tightened on the thin, slippery rectangle of his phone and his heart gave a ferocious thump. "Mr. Allbright. It's good to hear from you."

"I'll get right to the point. Your contract is approved. We'll get all the paperwork figured out soon, but I wanted to let you know myself."

Nathan slumped back in his seat, his ears buzzing. He'd done it. He'd landed the biggest client Nechako Industrial Supply had ever had, basically guaranteeing his promotion. Everything he'd wanted for so long was right there, at his fingertips.

So why wasn't he dancing around his desk? Why wasn't he shouting for joy?

"Nathan? You still there?"

"Yes, of course." He worked saliva into his arid

mouth. "That's great news. Thank you so much for calling me yourself."

"Julius and I were very impressed by your presentation. And by you. If you ever want a change from working for NIS, be sure to give us a call."

Startled and stunned by that unexpected stamp of approval, Nathan managed to stutter his way through the rest of the conversation, setting up the meeting required to make Allbright's announcement official for the next day.

He laid his phone on the desk as if it were made of glass and poked cautiously at his emotions.

He'd delivered what he'd promise. Melanie would be thrilled, as would Larry Manganeta, the head of the Western Canadian division of Nechako Industrial Supply—and the man in charge of hiring for the Vancouver Island sales manager position. Nathan had spoken to him earlier that day, setting up an interview via video conference on Friday. Even though he hadn't been able to give the other man any news about Mount Morgan at the time, the executive had been flatteringly confident that Nathan would deliver the goods.

Now he had. And he had no idea how he felt about it.

Hours later, Nathan pulled into his driveway and paused to let the garage door raise. Melanie had been as excited as he'd expected when he told her, and her jubilation had brightened his mood. Still unbalanced by his own reaction, though, he'd escaped her office as soon as he could while politely rejecting her suggestion of a celebratory drink after work.

Megan and Nora came out of Helen's house, Helen following. As he gathered his portfolio, laptop, and lunch bag, Megan buckled Nora into her car seat and took her place behind the wheel. Helen stood on her lawn, waving goodbye as the short strands of her hair gleamed silver and platinum in the late afternoon sun. The tall elm behind her fluttered its leaves, offering its own goodbye, the colourful flowers—petunias? geraniums?—circling its base nodding in the slight breeze.

God, he'd missed her. Missed talking to her, touching her. Just the sight of her made him feel centered, grounded. He needed to be with her. Now.

Chapter Fifteen

Nathan stacked his work paraphernalia on the cleanest part of the garage floor and exited through the big door. Helen hadn't moved from her place on her lawn. She waggled her fingers, and his heart leaped, pathetically pleased at the wordless invitation.

"How was your day? Have a good time with Nora?" His dress shoes clicked on the concrete of her driveway and sweat sprang up under his arms when he stepped into the full glare of the sun.

"Always." Helen's mouth curved up, laugh lines bracketing her lips.

He joined her in the shade of the tree and blinked, getting his first good look at her face. "I didn't notice before…"

Her forehead crinkled, and then her smile grew. "Oh my god, I'd forgotten. Helen wanted to play spa again."

Turquoise blue eyeshadow caked her lids and clumpy black mascara clung to her lashes. Blush darkened her usually pale cheeks to a garish red, and the equally scarlet lipstick had been generously smeared outside the lines of her lips.

"I see." He cleared his throat and bit his lip. *Do not laugh. Do not laugh.*

"I look like a demented clown." She widened her

eyes and stretched her lips in a frightening caricature of a happy expression, completely unembarrassed to be caught in public displaying a makeover by a four-year-old.

He choked, his chest fizzing, and let his laughter ring out. After the tensions of the day, it felt amazing, and contentment flooded through him. Between snorts, he managed to say, "Can I come over tonight? I've missed you."

Helen's chuckles faded away, and a shadow of vulnerability flitted behind her gaudy mask. "I've missed you, too."

"Good," he said with satisfaction, and warmth returned to her eyes.

"Meet you out back in five?" She gestured to her face with both hands. "Maybe a little longer. I have to get this off, and that might take a while."

When he climbed the stairs to her deck a few minutes later she was waiting for him, her skin scrubbed and glowing, two glasses of white already poured. He chose the seat next to her on the outdoor sofa and she curled her feet under her and leaned her head on his shoulder. The position was fast becoming one of his favourites. For the first time in hours he felt settled inside his skin, his heart rate steady and sure.

"So, you had visual proof of how my day went," she said. "How was yours?"

Her question caused a blip in his contentment. She'd never been anything but supportive of his goals, but that was when they were still only possibilities. Would her feelings change when she heard the news he had to share?

Did he want it to? What would he do if she asked him not to go? Not that he thought she would, but what if she did?

"My interview is scheduled for Friday." He kept his voice casual as he continued. "And I got a call from Stanley Allbright. Mount Morgan has accepted the proposal." His stomach plummeted as if he'd jumped off a diving board and he held his breath.

Helen stilled for an instant, and then dropped her feet to the deck and swivelled to face him. "Congratulations!" Pride shone in her bright eyes and her face stretched in a wide grin. He had to be imagining there was an echo of sadness under her sincerity. "I knew you would do it. You must be beside yourself."

"I'm not quite sure what I feel." He rolled his shoulders restlessly. "I should be over the moon, but I think I'm still in shock." It was natural he'd feel out of sorts until he came to terms with the change this meant for his life.

"Nathan." Helen took his chin in her fingers, her touch cool, and shook his head gently. "You've wanted this promotion a long time, worked so hard for it. Make sure you enjoy it."

"Don't get me wrong. I'm happy I signed the deal. It's the biggest of my career." Thoughts that had been swirling at the back of his mind since Allbright's call coalesced suddenly. "If I get the promotion, I won't be dealing directly with accounts anymore. I'll miss that, a lot. Many of my clients are friends as well as customers." Helen tilted her head, studying him intently, waiting as he thought through the nuances of his revelation. "My job is rewarding, challenging, and secure. As much as I want this promotion, it wouldn't be a disaster if I didn't get it."

"Maybe not. But you can't let change scare you away from your dreams. You deserve this, Nathan. Don't let anyone tell you differently, even yourself." She cuddled next to him again, her hand resting on his thigh.

Helen was right. Change was scary. But he didn't think fear had led him to this moment.

What if the lure of his long-held dream had blinded him to other paths? Sure, a promotion would be great. Being closer to his children and grandchildren would be fantastic.

But maybe the change he really wanted was sitting next to him right now.

Not getting the promotion also meant more time to explore Helen—her body, her mind, her soul. His stomach swooped with excitement...the excitement that had been missing after Allbright's call.

He needed to think. Today had been full of celebration and confusion. It was time to put it all aside and let his subconscious work.

Draping his arm over Helen's shoulders, he tucked her closer to his side. "I've done what I can," he said. "Now it's out of my hands. Until the interview, anyway." He leaned to place his still full wineglass on the low table at their feet. "Enough work talk. So, you missed me? How much?"

Helen put her own glass down, cupped her hand over his groin and gave him a challenging, teasing gaze. "This much."

Dinner was distinctly delayed.

Helen held her fingers to her lips as she watched Nathan return to his house later that evening. He'd kissed her with a tenderness that had brought the tears lying so close to the surface these days to her eyes. She'd blinked them away, determined he wouldn't see her distress, hiding it as she'd hid it since his announcement.

He was leaving her. She'd known it intellectually for weeks, but now she felt it in her bones, in her skin, in her very being. Every caress they'd shared when they'd made love before dinner had been one more step toward goodbye.

Obviously, expecting it to happen didn't make it any easier to accept. Not that she had a choice. Nathan would never refuse his dream, no matter how uncertain he'd seemed. He just needed time to get used to the idea. And so did she.

The next morning, she parked in her slot behind Golden Dragon Tattoos and prepared to face the other obstacle blocking her from the peace of mind she desperately craved. She glared at the brick wall in front of her, grey and nondescript and unoffensive, completely undeserving of her censure. It was nothing like the riotously painted windows at the front of the store. Sven was continually updating the glass mural, erasing designs no longer in style and adding new ones that showcased his abilities in glorious, oversize detail.

What would Golden Dragon be like without him? Bless his heart—he was the grumpy, arrogant soul of the business. Jamie was skilled and talented, but they didn't have the confidence or chutzpah Sven did, and neither did Helen.

Besides, she had no business training. How could she run one? And how could she take it on at all if cancer treatments were in her future?

As she readied the shop for the day's customers, she couldn't help but view everything from the perspective of owner. For example, she hated the cramped and dingy storage room, but Sven had always refused to let her reorganize and freshen it up. And when she'd been getting her own tattoos, she'd thought how nice it would be if the room were a little more feminine. Like a spa, with soothing colours and meditative music. Of course, the whine of the machine would drown that out, but it would still be nice in between applications.

Then she thought about licenses and taxes and employee insurance and scheduling staff and all the minutia that Sven currently handled. None of that sounded like fun.

It sounded like a challenge. One she desperately

wanted to take up.

Sven banged in a few minutes later. The rumble of his voice rolled up the hall, followed by the light tenor of Jamie's. They must have come in at the same time. Soon, two sets of footsteps approached, and she watched the entrance to the front room warily.

Sven stomped in and faced her across the counter as if he were a customer. Jamie, slight of build with a dark cap of hair and anxious hazel eyes, hovered behind him.

"So? You've had time to think. What's it going to be?" Sven's forceful bark no longer had the power to cow Helen.

She rolled her eyes at Jamie, and they grinned back. "Hello, Sven. How are you?"

He ignored her civility. "Stop making faces. India and I leave for Thailand in three weeks. We have to have this wrapped up before we go."

The biopsy results were expected any day now, but until then she had to keep stalling. "Are you sure you don't want me to manage the place while you're gone? Then when you come back you can take over again."

"I want out, free and clear. I told you before, my days of doing good work are numbered, the way my hands are going. Jamie is ready to take over."

Jamie leaned around Sven's huge form. "I'm not sure—"

"Well, I am." Sven's tone brooked no argument and Jamie subsided.

The trouble was, Helen agreed with Sven. "It's not you I'm worried about, Jamie. You are amazingly talented and will only get better. I'm the weak link here." In more ways than one.

"If I didn't know better, I'd think you didn't want to buy the shop." Sven's brows lowered menacingly over his narrowed eyes.

"I do. It's just—" Helen owed him an explanation. He was a good, though gruff, boss, and was offering her something he loved. She couldn't let him think she'd treat his baby with anything less than the respect it deserved. Besides, now that Megan knew, her secret was out.

"I might have cancer." Saying it fast didn't stop the horror from creeping across her shoulder blades. "I'll know for sure very soon. Please, can you wait a few more days?"

Jamie uttered a small squeak and Sven's frown deepened even more ferociously.

"Ah, for fuck's sake." Sven rounded the counter and enveloped her in a bear hug. For a moment she stood stiff and frozen, shocked by the unexpected embrace. She couldn't remember Sven even patting her on the shoulder. "I knew something was up when you had to change your schedule last week. Figured you'd tell me when you were ready."

Her arms slipped around his waist, and she pressed her cheek to his chest. He smelled of soap and shampoo and faintly of the sweat lingering from his morning workout. "I should have said something then."

"Nah. Your business is your business." His hand thudded against her back in a caress that knocked out her breath. Releasing her, he stepped back.

Jamie sidled into his place. Their hug was much gentler but no less sincere. "I can understand why you wouldn't want to commit to anything, not with that hanging over your head. What if..." They trailed away, their natural reticence taking over.

"What if what?" Sven had never let Jamie hide in the background, and obviously wasn't starting now.

"Well, I wouldn't mind learning the business side of things." Jamie bit their lip nervously. "I can't afford to buy it, but there's still time to teach me a lot before you go."

Still off balance from Sven's unconditional—and unexpected—support, Helen didn't grasp Jamie's point as fast as Sven did. She could only gape as the two persons discussed her future without waiting for her to catch up.

"Helen owns it, does what she can, you take over any other duties?" Sven's gravelly voice was as thoughtful as she'd ever heard it.

"Then, maybe, when Helen's ready to sell, I could take over." Jamie's shyness was fading fast in the face of Sven's approval.

"I like it." Sven nodded with all the royal benevolence of a Norse god.

It was time to regain control. "I still need a week. I can't, simply can't, make a decision today."

"Fine." Sven huffed a reluctant agreement. "But Jamie and I start training right away. Now, who have we got first?"

Chapter Sixteen

Nathan couldn't remember the last time he'd interviewed for a new job. He'd forgotten how nerve-wracking it could be. The distance created by the video conference did nothing to ease his tension and his leg jiggled uncontrollably. Thank goodness that giveaway tick was hidden from the camera's view.

Larry Manganeta, his solid, bulky torso encased in a too tight sport jacket, had been joined by two people from other sales regions and one from human resources. Larry and the woman from human resources sat at a conference table, a wood-panelled wall behind them. Nathan had a feeling the other two members—each in their own offices in Calgary and Edmonton—were there strictly to satisfy policy, as neither said a word after being introduced.

The woman from human resources led the interview, following what seemed to be a generic, impersonal script. After half an hour, Larry interrupted her with brisk impatience, and his first question was the one Nathan had been waiting for.

"What do you consider your biggest success as an account executive for NIS?"

Here we go. "I recently closed a seven-figure deal with Mount Morgan Mining." He didn't bother to hide his satisfaction and pride.

Larry leaned into his camera, his dark eyes piercing, thick black hair sweeping away from a low forehead. "It's done?"

"Signed on the dotted line yesterday." Despite his recent and unexpected ambivalence regarding the promotion, Nathan would always remember the thrill of watching Allbright slash his signature across the final page.

"Well done." Larry looked over his shoulder at the woman next to him. "As agreed?"

Her face pinched but she nodded. Larry turned back to the camera. "From the moment your CV hit my inbox, you have been my preferred candidate. When Melanie told me about the pitch you made to Mount Morgan, we decided to book your interview last to give you a chance to wrap that up. Since you have done so successfully, there is no reason not to move immediately to the next stage of the process."

The hairs on the back of Nathan's neck prickled and he drew air in through his nose.

"Nathan Spieth, how would you like to be the next Regional Sales Manager of Vancouver Island?"

Ever since learning she needed a biopsy, Helen had carefully nurtured a kernel of positive thought. Many breast lumps were benign, after all, and she'd done her best to visualize that as an end result. But all her hovering doubts and worries came to the fore with the phone call she received after lunch on Friday.

Jamie and Sven were tucked away in the miniscule office at the back of the shop. They had taken to spending every minute without a client together, Sven's gritty growl overriding Jamie's lighter tones as they worked their way through the operation of the tattoo parlor.

Helen wanted to believe Jamie had come up with

the perfect solution. But now, if she decided not to pursue ownership, she would have their disappointment to deal with as well. The weight of expectation already heavy on her shoulders grew with every passing moment.

Luckily, there was no one in the reception area when her cell phone rang, Dr. Chesley's name lighting up the screen. Helen watched it as she might a rattlesnake, and flinched when it rang again. With dread trickling down her spine, she answered.

Instead of Shelagh's calm tones, she was greeted by a preternaturally cheerful medical office assistant. "We're hoping you can come in on Monday to discuss your biopsy." She said the dreaded word as she probably said *cotton candy* or *kitten* or something else equally fluffy and sweet.

Helen's immediate, desperate thought was *I can't wait until Monday.* "Do you have the results back? Can't you tell me over the phone?"

"Dr. Chesley would like to check the surgical site, make sure it is healing properly. Also, she prefers to have further discussions in person."

"How about this afternoon? I can come right now." Helen scanned the empty front room with sightless eyes. Sven would just have to lump it if she left.

"I'm afraid she's unavailable. She's in surgery with another patient. Normally she's not in the office until eight on Monday, but she said she'd come in fifteen minutes early to meet you. Does that work?"

Lips numb, Helen gave a faint affirmative and disconnected the call.

She operated the rest of the afternoon on autopilot, greeting clients and taking payments with a forced and frozen smile. Thank goodness she wasn't asked to do any tattooing—she probably would have scarred her clients for life, and not the way they'd intended.

Her every breath beat with a terrifying refrain.

I have cancer. I have cancer.

It was the only explanation she could think of for the delay. If the biopsy had been clear, surely Shelagh would have told her right away. She had to know how worried Helen was. But if it were bad news, she wouldn't want to give that over the phone. That would be too harsh.

Like there was any way to soften the blow, Helen thought bitterly.

As Nathan drove home Friday afternoon, raindrops spattered sporadically onto his windshield. Towering grey clouds loomed in the distance, filling the sky over the rolling hills to the west of the city. Maybe the weather forecasters would be right for once. They'd called for thunderstorms every day for a week, but none had materialized yet, and the scorching heat had yet to break.

He was passing a transport truck on the double-lane highway when the hands-free system showed an incoming call from Greg.

His sons knew his interview had been that morning and were probably wondering why he hadn't contacted them as soon as it was over. Still reeling from the events of the day, Nathan's instincts screamed he should talk with Helen before anyone else, but maybe his sons deserved to hear the news first.

He tapped the screen. "Have you been designated the family spokesperson, Greg?"

His son chuckled. "I guess so. I'm not sure why. Both Lorne and Lyle have more time than me, especially in July." Wanda had passed on her green thumb to their middle child. Given the mild climate of Vancouver Island, Greg's plant nursery was always active, but Nathan assumed things ramped up during the warmer months.

"Lyle's probably pretty busy, too. Summer must be a high time for teaching surfing." At least, he imagined so. A born and raised landlubber, he had no idea how the seasons might affect his son's...career. Nathan squirmed at the gnawing feeling he was losing touch with his boys. He would have to fix that.

"Well, whatever the reason, I'm the one nominated. So—how did it go?"

The raindrops were heavy enough now Nathan had to turn on the windshield wipers. "They offered me the job."

"Awesome!" Greg's excitement pierced Nathan's heart. "It will be so great to have you live here. The baby's almost crawling, and you haven't seen her since she was a newborn. Not to mention Lorne's kids. He's registering Little Lorne for hockey this fall."

"It has been too long since I've seen you all, and I'm sorry about that. I will definitely make the time soon." Nathan took a deep breath. "But I won't be moving to the Island, Greg. I turned down the promotion. I'm staying in Prince George."

Helen paced back and forth in front of the large window in her living room, worrying at a hangnail on her thumb. The skin tore.

"Damn. Ouch." Blood welled and she hurried to the kitchen for a tissue, and then back to the window to keep watch.

She needed to talk to Nathan. She only wished it were for a happier reason. The news she had to share made her queasy with fear and regret and sorrow.

I have to break it off with him. Her arms wrapped around her middle, the pain of her decision so visceral it threatened to burst out of her gut. *It is the right thing to do.*

Outside the window, the breeze was picking up. The leaves on the enormous elm on her front lawn fluttered, the lighter undersides flashing like glimpses of goldfish in a pond. Raindrops darkened the heat-baked asphalt to a shiny obsidian. Finally, Nathan's SUV pulled into his driveway and disappeared into his garage.

If she hadn't received the distressing phone call from Dr. Chesley's office, she might have had more energy to spare to consider how his interview had gone. Not that it mattered. Whether he was leaving for Vancouver Island or not, she couldn't ask him to go through everything her diagnosis would entail.

Which left her one option.

For a moment she wished their roles were reversed. Not that she wanted Nathan to have the cursed disease—god, no!—but if he did, she would have stood by him. Just like she'd done with Aaron, she would have made the time they had together as good as she could, no matter what the potential outcome.

Because she loved Nathan. God knows when that had happened, but it had, and she was as certain of her feelings for him as she'd ever been for Aaron.

Which was why she had to end what they had together now. She'd have to be brutal about it. Nathan was a kind, caring man with a deep streak of loyalty and when she told him she had cancer, he'd feel obligated to support her. She couldn't do that to him. Couldn't let him put his life on hold yet again. Especially when what they had was so new, so fragile. Their temporary, mutually beneficial arrangement would never survive what was coming.

Watching Aaron fade with each passing day had been excruciating, but she was grateful they'd been given the time to say goodbye. They'd spent hours looking through old photo albums and reminiscing about holidays and family vacations and the many,

many joyful days they'd shared. Their decades of love and trust had made it possible for them to get through each day, a minute at a time.

She had accepted she wouldn't have that with Nathan.

I have to do the right thing. For him. She stepped outside.

Chapter Seventeen

Nathan tossed his briefcase onto the kitchen counter and strode to the front door. He had to see Helen, now. Had to tell her what he'd done.

He opened it with a tug and jolted with surprise when he saw her on his front step. It was as if his need had conjured her into being. "Helen! I was just coming to see you." In the scant time since he'd parked his car the desultory rain had morphed into a downpour. "Quick, get inside. You're getting soaked."

She slipped past him, the dampness intensifying the cucumber scent of her shampoo. Desire stirred in his groin, but he suppressed it. They had too much to talk about before he could even consider *that* thought.

"Let's go in the living room." He gestured and she walked through the opening that led to the formal space. He couldn't remember the last time he'd actually sat there. He split his time between the kitchen, his bedroom, and the study, where he had a TV, bar fridge and a recliner. What else did a man need?

This man needs Helen.

He still couldn't quite believe he'd turned down the promotion. When Larry had made his offer, it was as if a switch had flipped, convulsing Nathan with the force of a 120-volt current. Suddenly he could see his futures bright and clear—one with Helen, and one without. Larry had been stunned at his refusal, but Nathan had made a living trusting his gut, and his gut had shouted a resounding *no*.

Maybe all he'd needed was the validation of being offered the position. Turning his back on a dream he'd held for so long had been easy.

Much easier than leaving Helen.

She turned toward him, and his tumbling thoughts screeched to a stop at her set, intense expression.

"What's wrong?" His mind made a muscular leap, as if his brain had squeezed into a fist. "You got the results back." When he'd rejected the promotion, he'd known he was choosing a future that might involve a battle with cancer. His heart had made a simple calculation—any time with Helen was better than no time at all. He had hoped they'd have a day or two before having to deal with reality, though.

"Not officially." A bead of rain slid down the bridge of her nose and she swiped at it absently. "We need to talk."

The shoulders of her thin blouse and the flowery material of her skirt were damp with raindrops. Her hands clasped and unclasped in an uncharacteristically nervous tell.

Her agitation only amped up his anxiety. He wanted to take her in his arms, promise her everything would be okay, even if they both knew it might be a lie. "What's going on, Helen?"

"I think we should break up."

His lungs clogged for a suffocating instant, and then the air escaped with a frantic whoosh. "What?" Her statement was so far removed from his own thoughts he grew dizzy.

She lifted her chin and met his confused gaze. "I have an appointment with my doctor on Monday. She's going to tell me I have cancer."

Her confirmation of his deepest fears brought a sour taste to his mouth. He knew he had to say something, anything, but icy dread froze the words on his tongue.

"I appreciate everything you've done and said during the last weeks." Her smile lifted one corner of her mouth, as if she were too tired to raise both. "But I can't ask you to go through this again. It wouldn't be fair."

He shook his head, hoping to clear out the buzzing sensation filling his ears. It didn't help. "I don't understand."

"What's to understand?" Helen paced to the gas fireplace and laid one hand on the mantle, standing with her back to him. "I have cancer. You've been a good friend, but this would be above and beyond the call of duty." She paused, sucking in a breath, and then continued, her voice low and choked. "It's best if we don't see each other anymore."

"Friend? You think that's all I am?" He'd discarded his promotion, betting she would love him back. If not today, then someday soon. Only hours later, she was severing their ties.

She turned to face him, her shoulders held back in military precision. "That's what we agreed, isn't it? Friends with benefits?" This smile was wider than her first, but her eyes were glassy, unseeing. "I don't see the benefit for you anymore, so it's time to end it."

"Damn the benefits, Helen." He strode toward her and gripped her upper arms. "You need me for more than sex. I know you do."

"It's okay, Nathan, really. I told Megan about the biopsy, so she knows this is coming. Sven and Jamie at Golden Dragon know, too. And I have the Silverberries, thanks to you."

He froze. He'd done this to himself. He'd encouraged Helen to share her worries with others, because he'd wanted her safe and cared for when he left. Was it any wonder she was breaking it off with him now? She had no expectations that he'd stay.

"This is for the best, Nathan." Helen's tone was gentle yet firm. "You can go on with your life without all my messy problems."

He wanted to shake her until her teeth rattled, and his intensity frightened him so much he let her go and stepped back, hands raised. He could fix this. She didn't know his news yet. When he told her, she would understand. She had to. "I'm not leaving. I turned down the promotion."

Her eyes widened. "You what?"

"They offered me the promotion this morning, and I turned it down. I've already broken the news to my boys."

If anything, Helen looked more frantic, not less. "You can't do that. You have to call them, tell them you changed your mind."

"I can't. I won't." His gut cramped. He'd been so *sure*. The thought that Helen would push him away had never occurred to him. Which, now that he thought of it, was incredibly stupid. She'd been nothing but encouraging, had been instrumental in introducing him to Stanley Allbright and Julius Thames.

Oh, god, what had he done?

For long, painful moments he stared at her. He had so much to say the words jammed in his throat and left him speechless.

"I'm sorry, Nathan. So, so sorry." Helen's voice broke and she ran past. A moment later he heard the door open, the pounding of rain on the brick of his front path, the snick of the latch, and then humming silence.

She was gone.

Helen raced into her house and slammed the door behind her. Pressing against it, she moaned low and long, and then slowly slid down the panel to the floor, drawing her knees up into a ball.

It was raining so hard the short trip to and from Nathan's had soaked her to the skin. But it wasn't the chill from the deluge that racked her body with shudders.

She'd done it. She'd set Nathan free. But she'd been too late. She couldn't believe he'd turned down the promotion he wanted for so long. He'd sacrificed his dreams for her.

Her forehead pressed onto her knees, another moan escaping. She should have been strong enough to send him away weeks ago. Should never had given in to her need for comfort, for passion, for love.

She'd ruined everything, and now neither of them had anything.

She may have known him for twenty years, but it was only in the last two and a half weeks that she'd come to understand him. Not just because they'd had sex—although that certainly had something to do with it. It was impossible to hide your inner self when your outer self was bared and naked. She had hurt him— unintentionally, true, but that didn't make it better— and he'd forgiven her. He'd struggled with her potential cancer—and still stood by her side. They had shared days and hours and minutes together in ways they never had before—and she'd fallen in love.

It wasn't the same as in her twenties. Not better or worse, just different. They were both only fifty-five. In other circumstances, they could have had another twenty, thirty years, maybe even more.

She struggled to her feet, toed off her sandals and padded damply to her bedroom. In the en suite, she stripped and turned on the shower. Once the water was hot enough—punishingly hot, as she deserved— she stepped in.

It was time to get a grip. She wasn't giving up, not by a long shot. She and Shelagh would discuss treatments, and she'd do everything she was told. Breast cancer was beatable. Maybe in a year or so, when she had a better handle on how things were going, she could call Nath—

No. Thoughts like that were pointless. It wasn't only her cancer that stood between them, now. He would never forgive her for destroying his dreams. She'd never forgive herself, so how could she expect him to do so?

She had to let him go, well and truly.

Her tears mixed with the running water.

Chapter Eighteen

After learning of the biopsy, Megan had forced Helen to promise she would let her know the moment she had results. But her encounter with Nathan had left her soul torn and blistered, so she'd done nothing on Friday evening but huddle under a blanket while pretending to pay attention to whatever was on the television. Outside, lightning sparked and thunder boomed, so close at times the photos on her walls rattled and the lights flickered. The storm was still rumbling ferociously when she fell asleep.

She woke with the late dawn light shining in her eyes, a stiff neck, and an aching spine. For a single, stabbing moment she was back in the early days after Aaron's death, when she'd rouse in much the same state. Unwilling to sleep in their bed and needing the comfort of people, even if they were only two-dimensional representations on a glass screen, she'd spent much of that first terrible month drowsing on the couch.

Dragging herself to the kitchen, she prepped the coffeemaker. As she waited for it to drip through, she stepped onto her deck into a world that smelled so fresh and clean it was like breathing champagne. A gentle breeze caressed her, the early morning air vibrant on her skin. Despite the evidence of last night's storm in drenched cushions, broken branches, and scattered flower petals, she felt a rush of something too faint to call hope, but positive, nonetheless.

She may have lost Nathan, but she had survived tragedy before. Because of him she'd opened her heart and let others in. Sven and Jamie had become unexpected allies, and the Silverberries were proving to be more than casual acquaintances.

Somewhere along the way she'd also come to understand her own need for independence was rooted in a fear of rejection. If she didn't ask, then no one could say no. But time and time again recently she'd been proven wrong. She doubted she'd ever be completely comfortable with sharing every need and want, but that didn't mean she couldn't bend a little.

Speaking of which...

Nora was a notoriously early riser, so she had no compunction at texting Megan even though it was not yet seven o'clock. She kept it light and chatty, inviting the family over for dinner. Megan replied with acceptance for her and Nora but regrets from Nicholas as he was away at a dental conference.

Any news from the biopsy? Megan texted.

We'll talk tonight, Helen texted back. She waited, biting her lip, as the three dots flashed. But all that came back was a thumbs up emoji. With a sigh, she went to get her first coffee of the day.

Nathan was holed up in his study, sunk low in his favourite chair, feet on the coffee table. On the television, a commentator spoke in a low, soothing, British-accented voice. Golf was the perfect sport for moping—long moments of peace between short instances of intensity, with frequent replays so he didn't miss anything should he garner the enthusiasm to care.

Something was nagging him about Helen's announcement yesterday. Well, a lot of things were nagging him, but she had made one statement in particular that, in the confusion and agitation of the moment, he hadn't called her on.

It was hours after she left before he'd had the composure to recall the entire conversation. He'd been stretched out sleepless in his room, trying to forget the fact he'd made love to Helen in the very bed he was lying on, when it had come back to him.

I have an appointment with my doctor on Monday. She's going to tell me I have cancer.

Going to tell. Not *has told.*

What exactly did that mean? Helen wouldn't lie about something so important, so she must believe what she said. Of course, she could have been using it as an acceptable excuse to end their relationship, simply because she wanted out herself.

No. She wouldn't do that. Helen was a straight shooter. If she'd decided to end what they had, she'd tell him, not use a horrifying disease as a get-out-of-jail-free card. But it would be just like Helen to break it off with him because she thought that was what he wanted and was trying to spare him the decision. Regardless of what *she* needed. What *she* wanted.

Once he'd clarified that, he'd turned to examining his feelings about the promotion. If he'd refused it because of Helen and she was serious about breaking off their relationship, then he'd given up the promotion for nothing. He should be feeling intense regret at missing out on his dreams a second time.

He wasn't. He felt nothing but relief and a slight remorse at disappointing his sons. All these years he'd blamed Wanda for shortchanging his career, and now he'd done it to himself and was happy about it. He offered up a silent apology.

As he wasted the day watching grown men chase a

little white ball, one conviction grew stronger.

His love for Helen had flared from an ember of friendship and loyalty and passion that was stronger than any challenges it might face. He wasn't about to let her go at the first bump in the road. He needed to confront her about last night. If the ambiguity he'd spotted meant what he thought it meant, she wasn't going to get away with it.

He wasn't fooling himself about what the future might hold. How could he when he'd already lived through this scenario once? If she did have cancer, the road would be treacherous and fraught with peril. But the thought of Helen walking it alone made him sick to his stomach. She'd said she would be fine, relying on her friends and family to support her, but that wouldn't be enough.

She needed *him*.

Whether she knew it or not.

Nora built a complicated structure out of Lego blocks as Megan and Helen sipped their after-dinner wine on the couch.

Telling Megan had been both distressing and comforting. For one thing, her daughter had called her out on her pessimistic outlook. It had been her constant refrain all evening, and she continued it now.

"I know waiting is painful." She kept her voice low out of deference to Nora. Helen gave thanks her granddaughter was too young to catch the nuances in the conversation. "But I honestly think you've jumped to the wrong conclusion. Or at the very least, an unwarranted one. It's common practice not to give results over the phone."

Helen gave a tired nod, hoping this wordless response would be enough. Further argument was pointless. She and Megan were only repeating themselves, and she was exhausted.

More than a tiny part of her hoped Megan was right, and Helen *had* overreacted. But that hope was dangerous. While she'd give almost anything to have her verdict overturned, choosing to believe the news would be positive and then having the guillotine drop would be harder to take.

"Gramma! Look what I made!" Nora sat on her heels and beamed at the gravity-defying architectural marvel she'd created.

"That's lovely, sweetie. Good job." A crushing weight made it hard for Helen to breathe. She'd promised herself that, if her instincts were right and she was given the diagnosis she expected, she'd do her best to remain positive. Moments like these were precious, and she intended to store them up for the dark days ahead.

"Let's help Gramma clean up, and then we should head home." Megan wrapped an arm around Helen's shoulders and whispered in her ear. "Unless you'd like us to stay? Nicholas doesn't get home until tomorrow afternoon."

Helen shook her head. "I'll be fine. And I expect you to bring Nora on Wednesday as per usual." No matter what happened at Monday's appointment, she doubted any treatments would be in motion two days later.

"Of course."

A few minutes later Helen waved goodbye to Megan and Nora after giving each a longer hug than usual. She waited until the car was out of sight, and then turned to go in. A flash of movement caught her attention.

Nathan stood in the shadows between their houses.

Every cell in her body cried out for him, to run to him and have him wrap her in his arms and make it all go away. Her need was so fierce it froze her in place.

As he strode forward, she told herself she should race inside, lock the door. Because if he got within reach, she didn't think she could keep her promise to give him his freedom.

Chapter Nineteen

Helen stood framed in her doorway, the brighter light from inside the house forming a nimbus around her.

He knew the moment she caught sight of him. One hand raised, froze, and then dropped to her side. As he neared, he noted her pale face, her red-rimmed and shadowed eyes.

His need to take care of her was a physical ache. If he'd ever doubted his own feelings, he had none now.

She didn't move as he approached, other than a slight widening of her tired eyes and the flex of her throat as she swallowed. He came to a halt in front of her and stood silent for a breath, readying for the confrontation to come.

"You lied." Nathan kept his accusation gentle.

Her tightly pressed lips dropped open in a shocked O. "I did not."

He was pleased to see a glitter of green fire light her irises. "You lied by implication. You told me you had cancer. You don't know that for sure."

He read her admission in the slump of her shoulders, yet she still faced him with defiance. "I just spent the last few hours arguing with Megan about the semantics, and I won't spend the next few doing the same with you. When a doctor won't announce the results over the phone, it is reasonable to make the conclusion I did. I know I'm right."

He stepped forward and she held her ground. She stood on the slightly raised door sill, which made her almost eye-level with him. Her breath fanned his face, and he caught the scent of rich red wine and spicy spaghetti sauce. "I don't care."

He'd surprised her again. He could tell by the flicker of her eyelashes. "What do you mean?"

"I don't care if you have cancer. I don't care about furthering my career. None of that matters. All I want is to be with you."

A car whooshed by on the street behind him, thumping bass thudding in his ears for an instant. Or maybe that was his pulse, racing to the anxious beat of his heart. If Helen sent him away, he would have to respect her decision. At least for now. He waited, trying to still the nervous twitching of his fingers against his thigh.

Helen backed away and for a moment he feared she would slam the door in his face. Instead, she jerked a thumb over her shoulder. "Do you want to come in for a minute?"

Her tone wasn't exactly welcoming but he would take what he could get. He stepped in and she shut the door behind him with a gentle click before heading to the kitchen. He followed, formulating his argument.

Helen's mind whirled. Why wasn't he angry with her? He should be furious for so many reasons. But she'd read the truth in his eyes when he'd declared he wanted to be with her.

Afraid to trust what her heart was saying, she took a seat in the corner of her sofa. The cushion dipped as he lowered himself beside her. "I think we need to make a few things clear."

The back of her throat was tight and hot with hope and fear. Unable to look him in the eyes, she nodded.

"One." He took her hand. "Cancer or no cancer, I'm here for you."

A tiny sob escaped despite the leash on her emotions, but she'd shed enough surreptitious tears while Megan and Nora had visited and had no more left to give.

"Two." He interlaced his fingers with hers. "I gave up the promotion because it was the right thing to do. For *me*."

She couldn't let that blasphemy go by unremarked. "It wasn't. It couldn't be. You've wanted it for so long, worked so hard to get it. How could refusing it be the right thing? If my health issues in any way influenced your decision, I will hate myself."

"Ah." He tipped her chin up with his free hand. "There's one more thing you should know."

"Don't give me hope, Nathan," she begged. "I won't survive if you give me hope and then take it away."

"Helen." His voice was as gentle as the touch of his fingers on her hair. "I love you. And that is not going to change."

"Oh, god." She closed her eyes.

"That's not the reaction I was hoping for."

Was that amusement she heard? Her eyelids popped open, and she frowned. "Are you *laughing* at me?"

"You have to admit, this situation is pretty ridiculous."

"This is *serious*, Nathan. I have"—at his sternly pointed finger and fierce expression she corrected herself with a martyred sigh—"I *may* have cancer. You just gave up your dream job and probably ticked off your bosses in the process. What is so funny?"

"I thought by this stage in my life I'd be past all the drama. It's either laugh or cry, and I'd much rather laugh."

Helen knew exactly what he meant about the drama. After Aaron died, she'd grown to believe she'd reached a plateau in her life, that she would spend the rest of her days floating along, filling time with casual interests and family events. Now she was having a medical crisis, being urged to invest in a tattoo parlor, and was loved by a sexy, kind man.

Said man was staring at her with desire in his eyes, humour twisting one corner of his mouth. "What do you say, Helen?"

"We should wait until Monday." Desperation tinged her words. "Don't tell me you love me until after Dr. Chesley confirms the diagnosis, one way or the other."

"Too late for that, isn't it? I love you, Helen, and I'd like to hear you say it back."

She shook her head frantically. "I can't. Not until I know what's going to happen."

"Don't you see? We *never* know what's going to happen. No matter what your doctor tells you Monday, Tuesday I could get hit by a bus." Helen flinched and Nathan added hurriedly, "You know what I mean. We can't live our lives worried about what might happen at some time in the future."

"I never used to be like this," she said wistfully. "I used to take each moment as it came, certain there were good times ahead, ignoring the possibility of bad times. I don't know what's changed."

"You have a better understanding of how fragile life is." Nathan took her hand in both of his and pressed her cold fingers. "We've each lost people we loved. And we will again, there's no avoiding that. But it doesn't mean we should stop enjoying the days in between."

She had to be certain. "Promise me you're telling the truth about giving up the promotion. That it is what you want, regardless of what happens between us."

He answered with no hesitation. "I promise."

The band around her chest loosened. She flung herself into his lap and wrapped her arms around his shoulders, pressing her face into the curve of his neck. "I love you, Nathan. I didn't want to, but I can't help myself. I feel so selfish, needing you so much."

"Never feel that way. I love you, too." A tremor shook his body, and she heard him swallow. "We'll get through this. And we'll do it together."

Chapter Twenty

The doctor's receptionist made no comment when Nathan followed Helen into the exam room. Not that it would have mattered if she had. He was coming in, hell or high water.

It struck him that maybe Helen was right, that the doctor was about to confirm she had cancer, and that was why the receptionist hadn't raised a fuss. Icy needles raced up his chest to his cheeks and he closed his eyes to fight off the dizziness. When he opened them, Helen was seated on one of the cloth-covered, stainless steel visitor's chairs next to the paper-covered table. He dropped into the other and took her hand. Her fingers were lifeless in his grip and he felt a chill of premonition.

Shuffling the chair a centimetre closer, he perched tensely with his thigh pressing Helen's. He had the insatiable urge to jiggle his knee but forced it to remain still. He had to at least appear steadfast and confident for her sake.

She'd been scarily calm since waking in his arms this morning after falling asleep around four. He'd known the time because he hadn't been sleeping either, barely dozing through the dark hours. He'd let her sleep as long as possible, but the appointment was for 7:45 am and he'd kissed her awake with regret.

He slid a glance at her face. She was pale and

composed, her silver hair neatly combed, makeup discreet and flattering. No one looking at her would realize she was about to hear life-changing news.

After their cathartic conversation on Saturday night, he'd left the subject of cancer alone. It was pointless to argue further, and Helen needed his support, not his criticism.

But *god*, did he hope he'd be able to say *I told you so* in a few minutes. Not that he would. He just wanted to be *able* to.

"Thank you." Helen's voice was quiet yet firm. "Thank you for coming with me today."

"Of course." He'd emailed Melanie Devane to let her know he wouldn't be in until Tuesday. If Helen were right, he couldn't leave her alone. If she were wrong—well, there would be some celebrating to do. Besides, he was in no mood to take the lambasting he was sure was waiting for him about the rejected promotion. "Where else would I be?"

"Nowhere." He was surprised to see a small grin lighten her face. "If I couldn't talk you out of loving me, I don't think I can talk you out of anything."

He smiled back. *We're going to be all right*, he thought with relief. No matter what happened next.

Helen didn't know what she'd done to deserve Nathan's love, but she hoped she'd never do anything to lose it. Despite her best efforts to push him away, he had refused. Either she hadn't tried hard enough, or he was too stubborn.

Probably a bit of both.

She drew in a breath to the depths of her belly, eased it out through pursed lips, and her heartbeat slowed. Nathan's fingers were warm on hers and she twisted her hand to interlace them, his presence comforting, his touch a balm.

Shelagh would be in soon. They'd been told by the cheerful receptionist that Dr. Chesley was running a couple minutes late, but not to worry, and a few moments ago Helen had heard Shelagh's familiar tones through the thin walls of the exam room.

Not to worry. Hah. All Helen had done for almost three weeks was worry. She'd just managed to hide it better some days than others. No matter what the result of the biopsy, it would be a relief. Then she could start making plans, get her life organized— whether it was for treatments or buying Golden Dragon—or both. The uncertainty was exhausting.

The door opened with startling abruptness and Nathan jerked, his shoulder bumping hers. Shelagh entered the exam room with brisk steps, heels tapping, and shut the door. She gave Nathan a narrow-eyed stare.

"And who have we here?" Her gaze dropped pointedly to their clasped hands.

"Nathan Spieth. I'm Helen's..." He trailed off, sliding Helen a sideways glance.

"Boyfriend." The word was ridiculous, with elementary school yard connotations that did no justice to the depths of her feelings, but it was the best she could come up with. Nathan's eyes lit with warmth and humour and he squeezed her fingers, as if he were in on the joke.

"I see." Shelagh's focus flicked from Helen to Nathan and back again.

Worried she was going to suggest Nathan leave, Helen said, "I want him here. I can't do this alone." *And I don't have to*, she thought with dizzy relief. *How amazing it that?*

Wrinkles creased Shelagh's forehead. "It's a routine examination of the surgical site. If you're not suffering any pain or inflammation there's no need for worry."

For god's sake get on with it. The voice in Helen's

head was shrill. She took a deep breath to make sure her next words were calm and rational. "No, I'm feeling fine. That's not what's important, anyway. I've waited long enough, Shelagh. It's cancer, isn't it?"

In all the years they'd known each other, Helen had never seen Shelagh gobsmacked. There was no better word to describe the look on her doctor's face. "Didn't Mindy tell you?"

Helen assumed Mindy was the irritatingly smiley receptionist. "She refused to tell me anything other than I needed to come see you."

"The biopsy was clear. No cancer. We have a confirmed diagnosis of sclerosing adenosis, a benign tumour."

"Oh." Helen swayed and Nathan wrapped his free arm around her shoulders. "No, she didn't tell me that."

"I am so sorry." Shelagh crouched at Helen's knees and clasped her hands around Helen and Nathan's. "I wanted to give you the good news myself on Friday but got called into emergency surgery with another patient. I didn't want you to wait any longer, so I told Mindy to let you know the results and that I would give you more details today. I *certainly* didn't want to cause you more stress. My sincere apologies."

Helen heard Shelagh as if she were speaking from the far end of a long tunnel. She knew she should be furious at the cheerful but apparently incompetent medical office assistant. But all she could take in right now were those sweet, sweet words.

No cancer.

Shelagh was still talking, something about further checkups and how sclerosing adenosis was often mistaken for cancer which was why a surgical biopsy was the favoured method of diagnosis. Helen hoped Nathan was paying attention because all she wanted to do was bask in how wrong she'd been.

How *wonderful* it was to be wrong.

Chapter Twenty-One

The shrieks and squeals of grown adults echoed from the lake shore up the steep incline to the deck where Nathan sat beside Helen in mismatched loungers holding hands like teenagers. A glass with the dregs of her signature Red Shoe Martini in it rested on the planks beside her. He sipped the last of his beer and put it down gently.

How different this meeting of the Silverberry Book Club would have been if Helen's tumour hadn't been benign. Not just for him and Helen, but for all the members. Over the years they'd become good friends, almost family. They would have been distraught if the diagnosis had gone the opposite way.

Last weekend's thunderstorm had cleared the air, and sunshine had descended once again, bringing back soaring temperatures and blue skies. The book discussion had lasted about fifteen minutes before being abandoned for the lure of crystal-clear water and paddle boards, kayaks and sunbathing.

"Lynn seems nice. Where did you meet her?" Nathan let his gaze rest on Helen. She was stretched out, eyes closed, looking as relaxed as he'd seen her in years. Her navy-blue bikini celebrated the mature curves of her body—a body he was getting to know very well.

She answered without opening her eyes. "She came in for a tattoo. We chatted while I inked her, and I thought she'd be a good fit."

Given Lynn's laughter ringing from below, Helen had been right. The joyful sound mixed with Terrance's deeper chuckles as Penta shouted instructions to Stephanie, who was trying to stand on the paddle board. Frequent loud splashes indicated her lack of success.

"When is the sale final?" Helen had wasted no time telling Sven the good news of her diagnosis and the paperwork to transfer ownership of Golden Dragon had been drawn up immediately.

"Next week. It's all with the banks and lawyers now." Helen's hands twitched as if she couldn't wait to get started. He knew she was nervous about the new challenge but had no doubt she'd make a success of it. It was going to be a summer of new beginnings, for both of them.

He had no regrets about turning down the Vancouver Island job. His sons had been gratifyingly disappointed with his decision, and he'd had to promise frequent visits to appease them. Telling them about Helen had distracted them nicely, however. To a man they'd been shocked and surprised at his relationship with the woman they'd known most of their life as Mrs. Mansfield. But after they'd had a chance to absorb his announcement, they'd seemed pleased to accept her new role.

Nathan's eyes drifted to the tiny biopsy scar almost hidden by the edge of Helen's bikini bra. He had lavished many kisses on it in the last week—along with every other inch of her body—and yet still hadn't reassured himself she was well and whole.

"It sounds like everyone is enjoying themselves," Helen said, her lids lifting languidly to uncover her clear green eyes. "We should do this all the time."

"It might not be quite the same in December."

She grinned. "True." With a satisfied sigh she rose on her elbows and shifted higher in the lounger. "There are lots of interesting things to do in the winter, though. Not that reading books isn't interesting, but maybe we can spice things up with different activities, too."

"I'm up for that. And given the commotion below, I think everyone else will be, too."

Helen's entire being radiated joy and contentment and energy. She'd always appeared to savour life, but the last few days he'd sensed a new appreciation, a deeper enjoyment of every moment. It was a sensation he shared—as if the air was spicier, the sun brighter, his skin more sensitive.

"Do you want to go down and join them?"

Something in Helen's tone raised the hairs on the back of his neck. She regarded him with wide-eyed innocence—and then licked her lips with sultry invitation. "Do you?" he said, his voice hoarse.

She reached behind her and unhooked the back of her bikini and his tongue went numb. Then she shrugged it off and her breasts were bare to the summer sun and he had to hold onto the arm of his chair to keep from grabbing her.

"Not really," she said. "I think I need to lie down for a little while." She stood up, keeping her back to the water though the angle of the slope to the shore hid her from any eyes that might be looking their way. Her bikini top dangling from her hand, she crooked her finger. "Coming?"

Helen's heart raced as Nathan scrambled with satisfying haste off his lounger and followed her into the cabin. While the weeks before her diagnosis had moved with agonizing slowness, the last few days had been a whirlwind. Sven was eager to complete the sale so he and India could fly off into the sunset. Megan had shown her relief in frequent phone calls and extra visits with Nora. The Silverberries had declared today's meeting a celebration.

As for Nathan...

She swayed her hips provocatively as she led him down the narrow hall. He'd barely left her side, other than for the time he spent at work, and while she felt a little guilty at the attention, she was also revelling in it.

It was time to reward him for how he made her feel.

In the bedroom she took his hand and swung him around so she could close the door. He wore loose swim trunks and his erection was evident, the tips of his ears and his cheekbones flushed from more than the sun.

"There's no lock." She tossed the bikini bra to the side and shimmied out of the briefs.

He shook his head.

"You'll have to hold it shut." She gestured him forward and indicated he lay a palm on the panel on either side of her head. His eyes were hot and heavy on hers. "Don't move."

She sank to her knees, and he groaned. He gave a second, louder growl when she slid her hands into his trunks and shoved them to his ankles. "Quiet, now. Someone might come into the cabin."

His cock bobbed as if the idea excited him. *Interesting. We'll have to talk fantasies soon.*

She buried her nose in the depression of his groin and breathed him in. Her blood swept thick and slow through her veins, heat gathering in her womb. The tips of her breasts brushed his thighs and she hummed.

When she took him in her mouth his hips thrust forward, but he remained silent. She gave his ass an approving pat and set to work, her goal to drive him so wild he'd forget his unspoken promise and shout loud enough the neighbours would hear, let alone the Silverberries.

Before long he was panting so deep and uneven she knew he was close. Bringing him to this fever pitch made her wet and she squeezed her inner muscles to ease the hollow achiness. As if sensing she was as close as he was, he gripped her biceps and dragged her to her feet, pressing her back against the door. Sweat had gathered between her breasts and in the creases of her knees and where their naked skin met she could feel a similar dampness on his body.

His hands cupped her jaw, and his tongue swept between her lips as if he wanted to taste himself in her mouth. She was dimly aware of when he kicked off his trunks but by now was in such a frenzy could barely tell where she ended and he began. He bent his knees to grip her thighs, lifting and widening her so he could slide home, filling her emptiness so completely she forgot her own instructions and gave a loud, appreciative moan.

They hadn't made love this way yet, and Helen was drunkenly thrilled to find they were a perfect match. He reached places inside her that set off sparks and explosions throughout her body. When she lifted one knee the sensations increased exponentially. "Hurry," she panted. "Yes. Like that. More."

He increased his tempo, reading her disjointed commands correctly. Every nerve in her body coiled tighter and tighter until she fractured like an exploding spring, her head thrown back, her mouth opened in wordless amazement. Dazed, she clung to his waist until three thrusts later he stiffened and arched, joining her in utter satisfaction.

Her chest rose and fell, matching Nathan's heaving breaths. "Now I *really* have to lie down." She muttered the words against the side of his neck, too exhausted to lift her head. Disengaging, they staggered to the bed and fell across it sideways. Helen threw an arm and a leg over him, cuddling in close, and he slid his arm under her shoulders.

"That was amazing. I can't believe we did it with guests nearby." Nathan sounded half-asleep and Helen grinned.

"I didn't know you had a discovery fetish." She toyed with the hairs on his chest, his heart pumping rapidly under her fingertips.

"I didn't, either."

She giggled. "It's nice to know there are still things to learn about each other."

His arm tightened. "I feel like I've learned more about you—about *us*—in the last three weeks than the last two decades."

"Me, too." She nuzzled her nose against his neck in agreement. "Just think what the next twenty years will teach us."

"I know one thing already." In a sudden surge that made her squeak, Nathan reared up and flipped her on her back, staring down with glittering eyes. "I love you."

Her belly warmed at the sincerity etched on his face. "And I love you. Thanks for not giving up on me."

"Never." His kiss was a promise. "We're never giving up on each other."

Acknowledgements

A special thank you to Amie Easton of JuggerBean Tattoos, for an enlightening and fun conversation!

And if you're interested, here's the recipe for Helen's Red Shoe Martini.

1.25 oz. vodka
.75 oz. sour raspberry liqueur
3 oz. cranberry juice
1 tsp. lime juice

Mix all ingredients. Can use a martini glass, but tastes just as good out of a tumbler. Yum!

Thanks for reading
Secrets Under the Covers.

Reviews and ratings are a great way to help other readers discover new authors. Just a line or two is all that's needed—or simply click the number of stars you think it deserves. I encourage you to post your honest opinion at the retailer where you purchased your copy, on GoodReads and BookBub. Thank you so much!

Visit my website to discover more titles in the Silverberry Seduction Seasoned Romance Series or keep reading to preview the first two chapters in *Loving Between the Lines (Book Two).*

LOVING BETWEEN THE LINES
(Silverberry Seduction, Book 2)

CHAPTER ONE

Lynn Kolmyn had *not* envisioned this on her first day back after a year of maternity leave.

"I am so sorry." She stood in front of Cynthie Neal's desk, jiggling her wailing son on her hip. Her boss regarded her with raised eyebrows. Panic curdled her belly, and she swallowed. "The daycare had a flood overnight. They've promised me an alternate location will be arranged by tomorrow, but I had nowhere else to bring Oscar today."

Cynthie's matte red lips pressed into a thin line. "As we discussed, I'm not totally adverse to having children at the office for short periods of time, but I don't see how you, or anyone else, will get any work done with this"—she waggled her fingers in Oscar's direction—"going on."

Lynn couldn't blame her. Her son's protests had risen in volume since she'd stepped into the room. The back of her throat burned with frustration.

"Give me one minute." Hurrying to her desk, one of two in the outer office, she scrabbled through the backpack she'd tossed beside it, searching for the baby biscuits she'd shoved in it this morning.

At the other desk, Sarah Little watched, a sympathetic expression on her round, cheerful face. "Need some help?"

Lynn pulled out the foil package and held it up triumphantly. "Got it." She smiled her thanks at Sarah's offer and hustled back to the inner office. Plopping into the visitor's chair, she ripped the package open with her teeth, slid out a cookie, and handed it to Oscar. He grabbed it eagerly and shoved it in his mouth.

Silence fell. The tension banding across her shoulder blades eased a fraction.

She spit the corner of foil into her fist as discreetly as she could. "I feel terrible about this. I thought he'd be happy here for an hour or two. At least long enough for me to get up to speed so I don't waste more time tomorrow. I should have just called." When the daycare had notified her it was closed, delaying her scheduled return to work had seemed unsupportable and bringing Oscar with her the only choice.

Now the squalling had stopped Cynthie's pinched nostrils relaxed. "Yes, you probably should have." Her dry tone held little censure, though, and Lynn saw a gleam of amusement in the other woman's sharp blue eyes.

She slumped back in the seat, relief softening her spine. Thank god Cynthie was a strict but understanding woman. "I promise it won't happen again." It shouldn't have happened once, Lynn berated herself. She *always* had back up plans for her back up plans. But things had changed in the year since Oscar's birth. Some days she was thrilled to make it out of her pajamas, let alone make contingency plans for imaginary scenarios.

"I suggest you head home today and try again tomorrow. But since you're here, there is something I might as well mention." She picked up a pen and slipped it through her fingers, back and forth, back and forth. "The marketing coordinator for the Canyon Cats quit. Peterson Brewster asked if we could help out until a replacement is found. I want you to handle it."

Lynn's main duty as arena event director was to assist the businesses and organizations that rented the facility. Most of the concerts, trade shows, and sports tournaments were single night or once-a-year occurrences. Not so the Prince George Canyon Cats. The junior hockey team played more than thirty games at home from September to March—more if they made the playoffs. Not that they had in recent years, but that was beside the point. What with training camps and practices and other team events, the Canyon Cats were vital to the financial health of the arena—and as such needed to be kept happy.

"What about my regular duties?" The marketing coordinator was a full-time position. How could she add that to her plate and not become an absentee mom? She needed to work to support her son, but this was more than she'd been expecting. Mind you, she loved her job with all its challenges and her brain was already whirling with promotional ideas for the team, even as her stomach roiled at the thought of being away from Oscar longer hours.

Maybe she wouldn't feel so torn about the conundrum if she'd been in her twenties, but becoming a first-time mom at thirty-nine made every moment with him precious and fragile.

"Sarah can finish the projects she started while covering your mat leave and continue to pick up some of the slack. But it will require more time and effort, I know that. I can't see any way around it. We can't say no to Peterson." Cynthie aligned the pen on her desk perfectly with the edge of her blotter. "Hopefully he will hire someone within a month or so."

She nodded with resignation. "I'll make it work." She rubbed her chin on Oscar's head, inhaling his fresh scent. His hair was finally thickening, the reddish-brown showing a tendency to curl. Sticky fingers gripped her bare wrist, and her heart swelled at the innocent touch. How was she going to survive being away from him all day? "Thanks for the heads up. We can talk about it more tomorrow."

"Sounds good." Cynthie rose and Lynn followed

suit. Oscar wriggled restlessly and rubbed his eyes. "Looks like someone is ready for a nap."

"Yes." Neither of them had had a good sleep the night before, which might have accounted for his fractiousness this morning. "Again, I'm sorry about today. I promise to make up for it. See you tomorrow, Cynthie."

Benjamin Whitestone stepped into the concourse of the arena, closed the door to the Canyon Cats team offices behind him, and leaned against the red-painted brick wall. Pressing his fingertips into the rough surface, he squeezed his eyes shut and breathed deeply.

When Peterson Brewster had summoned him to his office, he hadn't been able to suppress the guilty feeling he'd done something wrong. He'd only been head coach of the Canyon Cats for two weeks. Logic dictated he had no reason to worry that his performance had been judged subpar already.

Logic hadn't stopped him from worrying before, and it hadn't this morning, either.

Turned out Brewster had just wanted to welcome him formally to the organization. He'd met the very involved owner during the hiring process, but he'd been out of town since Benjamin's return to Prince George. Now the meeting was over, he could concentrate on his next challenge—his first official practice. Training camp had ended, and the roster was set. The hardest work was about to begin.

Taking one last deep breath, he pushed off the wall and strode toward the stairs leading down to ice level. As he reached the door to the arena administration offices, it swung open. He dodged to avoid being struck by the heavy metal panel. A woman with her arms full of child stumbled into him.

"Careful now." He gripped her biceps to steady

her. Two black bags draped off her shoulders and the sharp corner of one thudded against his thigh as she spun around. He released her and rubbed his leg.

"Sorry." She shifted the baby to her other hip and gave him a quick, harried glance before focusing once more on the squirming, squawking bundle.

He'd had little exposure to children but given the length of the legs kicking at her thighs and the arms flailing about her head, this was no newborn. Other than that, he had no clue.

"I should have been more careful when I opened the door," the woman continued. "I hope I didn't hit you."

That voice. Husky and low, it evoked a sudden memory of subdued lighting, sultry jazz, and smoky whiskey. "Lynn?" His palms tingled, remembering the smooth curves of the shoulders he'd just been clutching.

Her chin lifted and their eyes met. For a moment, her expression remained blank. Then she blinked.

"Benjamin?" The baby continued to wriggle and wail and she bounced and jiggled in the age-old way of mothers everywhere. "What are you doing here?"

He could only stare. He'd thought of Lynn more often than a one-night stand deserved. Especially a one-night stand that had occurred two years ago. Of course, it had also been the day after his father's funeral. Maybe the pain of that time and the comfort she'd given him was why she'd stuck in his mind more than any woman he'd slept with—before or since.

She asked you a question. Answer, you dummy. "I'm the new head coach. Of the Canyon Cats."

Her eyes widened. "*You're* Benjamin Whitestone?"

In the dim light of the jazz lounge where they'd met—and later, in the hotel room he'd brought her to—he'd been too caught up in first misery and then passion to remember the colour of her irises, but saw now they were a bright pale blue. "Yes?" He couldn't help the upward lilt, though it made him sound like an idiot. Reeling from this unexpected encounter, he wasn't certain of anything, even his own name.

"I read you'd been hired, but I didn't realize *that* Benjamin was, well, *that* Benjamin."

Since they hadn't bothered to exchange last names at their first meeting that made sense. "I've thought of you. Often." The truth blurted out before he could stop it. "How have you been?"

Her eyebrows quirked up and she shifted the now restlessly dozing baby on her hip. "I'm doing well. This is my son Oscar. He's a year old. Just last week, actually."

His head spun, as if a giant defencemen had laid him out flat with a body check and his skull had bounced off the ice. Scrambling to do the math, he stuttered, "A year? And we...is he..."

"No." Her tone was firm and laced with amusement. "Relax. He's not yours."

"Oh." Surely the rush flooding his body was relief. He'd never wanted to have kids. He'd been a disappointment as a son and couldn't imagine what a mess he'd make of being a father. "So, you're married?" Oh, god. Had she been married when they'd had their night together? She'd said she was single— he remembered asking—but had she lied?

"Also no." The amusement was gone, exasperation in its place. "Before you jump to any more conclusions, let me explain. Though I can't see how it's any of your business." The baby—whose name he'd already forgotten—lifted his head from her shoulder and squawked. She cradled his skull in her hand and joggled rapidly. "I'm in a hurry to get home so he can have a proper nap, so you'll have to save any questions for later. I am not and never have been married. I wanted a child, so I did in vitro fertilization, starting the process a month after we...met. Oscar is the result of that process." The baby's squalling took on a frantic tone. "I have to go. Congratulations on the new job. Good luck."

Before Benjamin could say another word—which was probably for the best, given his foot-in-mouth disease—she was gone.

CHAPTER TWO

Benjamin trudged down the wide flight of stairs to ice level, stunned and dazed by the chance meeting. In his office, he retrieved his skates and hockey gloves. The players would be waiting in the dressing room, but he made his way to the home team's bench instead, needing a moment to settle himself.

He gripped the wide wooden edge of the rink boards. The glistening ice, smooth and unmarked by the lethally sharp skates soon to be powering across it, taunted him. Shaking off thoughts of Lynn, he focused on the reason he'd returned to Prince George.

A battle would be fought on this ice, and on ice just like it in arenas across Western Canada. A battle for redemption. A battle he had to win.

His heart beat heavily in his chest, thundering with the anxiety that was a long familiar companion. Others might view him as washed up at thirty-five, but he'd made a vow to stop thinking of himself that way and taking this job had been the first step.

"Ready, Coach?"

He turned to the man who had appeared at his side. Levi Ghostkeeper stared at him with challenge in his jutted chin and narrowed eyes. As assistant coach of the Prince George Canyon Cats for the past five seasons, people in the know—as well as Levi himself—had expected he'd fill the head coach position. Instead, Benjamin had been hired. Levi had made his displeasure clear from the moment of their introduction.

And continued to do so every chance he got.

"Let's do this." His fingers aching with tension, he released the rail and sat on the metal bench. Removing his shoes, he slid his feet into his skates and laced them up, the motions ingrained and automatic.

Levi vanished down the tunnel leading behind the bleachers, his shouts echoing off the concrete walls and floor. A surge of adrenalin made Benjamin's face tingle, and he lifted his chin to scan the empty arena.

Remembering the rush of six thousand fans cheering when he stepped on the ice, the hometown star that was going to set the hockey world on fire.

Remembering the boos and hisses when he'd failed them all.

Like a gathering storm, he sensed the approach of the young men that had been placed under his authority. Casual profanities and shouted insults, the soft thudding of skates on padded flooring and sharp creaking of protective gear, reached him before the first player came into view. Hiding his trembling fingers inside his bulky gloves, he stood between the metal bench and the wooden boards, nodding at those that made eye contact as they passed, making note of the ones that didn't. It was his job to meld them into a unit, from the sixteen-year-old rookies dreaming of national league glory to the twenty-year-old veterans learning to accept unwelcome reality.

And if he did his job right, give them all the chance to celebrate the success he'd denied himself.

The crisp sound of blades cutting ice did little to fill the huge space. Gazing up at the enormous score clock hanging from the rafters like a guillotine, Benjamin took a deep breath, squared his shoulders, and stepped through the gate, his skates as comfortable as slippers, his strokes swift and sure. He glided to a stop on the Canyon Cats logo in the centre of the ice and blew his whistle.

"Bring it in, boys. It's time to get to work."

Lynn didn't let herself be distracted by thoughts of Benjamin Whitestone until she had Oscar safely tucked in his crib at home. *Sorry, officer. I ran that stop sign with my baby in the back seat because I was reliving the hottest one-night stand I ever had.* That it was her only one-night stand was a moot point. The passion of those hours was seared into her very sinews.

What a morning. First the panicky call from her daycare provider about the flood, the impulsive and ultimately insane decision to bring Oscar to work, and the twist-of-fate meeting with a man who'd haunted her dreams for two years.

In the spare room that doubled as her home office, she unpacked her laptop from her messenger bag, determined to review emails while Oscar slept. Cynthie may have been understanding but Lynn held herself to a higher standard. One she'd completely failed to attain that morning.

Before settling to work, she went to the kitchen to refill her water bottle. As she held it under the stream from the tap, her eye caught the infinity symbol tattooed on her wrist. It was so familiar she rarely noticed it, but today it blazed off her skin like a beacon.

The day she'd had it inked had been the day she'd decided to skip the husband stage of her life plan and move onto the baby stage.

The night she'd had it inked was the night she'd slept with Benjamin. Now known as Benjamin *Whitestone.*

Though she'd been on maternity leave throughout the last hockey season, it had only been good business sense to keep up with the happenings of the organization that was her biggest client. She'd read little more than the headlines regarding the hiring of the new head coach, as in the normal course of events she wouldn't have had much interaction with any of the Canyon Cats on-ice staff. Now she was handling the team's marketing duties for at least a few weeks, she wouldn't be able to avoid them completely. And by *them* she meant Benjamin.

Snorting out a chuckle, she recalled the varied expressions that had crossed his face during their short encounter. He really had made an ass of himself, first in revealing his terror he might be a father, and then jumping to the assumption she was married. He'd given her the upper hand the next time they met. Not that she needed the upper hand. They were both professionals. There was no reason this had to be awkward, especially since she'd cleared up all his ridiculous misunderstandings.

It might still be a good idea to learn as much as she could about him. For business purposes, of course. Nothing personal, and certainly nothing to do with the sparks of lust fizzing in her veins as she relived their night together.

Back in her spare room office, she fired up her laptop and made her way to the website for the local television news station. A quick search brought up the story she wanted. It included a video, so she set it to full screen, plugged in her earbuds so as not to disturb Oscar, and hit play.

The sports reporter, a young man with dark hair and a strong nose, sat at the anchor desk, a graphic of the Canyon Cats logo over his shoulder. He announced the hiring, and then the shot was replaced with video of a hockey game as the anchor went on. "This will be Benjamin Whitestone's first head coaching position. It is also his return to his hometown. A star in the Prince George Minor Hockey Association, Whitestone was drafted by the Canyon Cats as a Bantam, playing his entire junior career here."

The video changed again to what appeared to be a post-game interview with an unbearably young Benjamin. His sweat-dampened dark hair clung to his forehead, where his helmet had pressed a red line into the flesh. The thin whiskers of an infant beard were scattered in patches across his cheeks. Lynn's heart clutched at the sight, not only at Benjamin's vulnerability but the foreshadowing of a teenage Oscar.

The sports reporter continued. "He held several team scoring records and is well-remembered for his blazing speed. But his most notable claim to fame—or maybe infamy—is for a missed penalty shot on home ice in the final game of the National Championships. A missed shot that cost the Canyon Cats the trophy."

He paused to let the highlight run uninterrupted. The footage from fifteen-or-so years ago showed Benjamin racing to a puck placed on the blue line, before slowing to bob and weave in an attempt to throw off the goaltender. His wrist shot, so quick she almost missed it, sent the puck sailing by the net, wide by at least a foot. The boos and jeers of the crowd rang in her earbuds, shocking in their animosity.

What a weight for a teenager to carry on his shoulders. Lynn couldn't help but feel sympathy for the young man Benjamin had been.

The video cut back to the reporter at the desk. "Whitestone's career in the NHL never matched the potential he'd shown as a junior. He played for five teams in six seasons, and then retired after a hit that gave him his third concussion. After playing in Europe for a short time, he returned to North America and became an assistant coach. Given the Canyon Cats' lacklustre results in the past three seasons, he will have to work miracles to get the team to the playoffs this year."

Lynn closed the video, pulled out her earbuds, and

sipped her water. She had a vague recollection of the championship the reporter had mentioned. At the time, she'd been concentrating on her university education with little attention to spare on junior hockey. If she had been more of a fan, maybe she would have recognized Benjamin that night at the jazz lounge. More than likely not—it was a decade and a half later, after all.

And now it's two years after that, she reminded herself. So many changes had happened between then and now, the most important of which was sleeping in the room next to her. She was a mother. Any relationship she might cultivate had to be good for Oscar, not just her.

Which meant another one-night stand was out of the question—no matter how much the idea tempted her.

***

Want more? Look for *Loving Between the Lines* in e-book and paperback at your favourite online retailer.

ABOUT THE AUTHOR

Brenda Margriet writes savvy, slow burn, contemporary romances with ordinarily amazing characters. In her own ordinarily amazing life, she had a successful career in radio and television production before deciding to pilfer from her retirement plan to support her writing compulsion.

Readers have called her stories "poignant," "explicit and steamy," "interesting, intriguing and entertaining," and "unlike any romance you've read before" (she assumes the latter was meant in a good way).

Brenda would love to stay in touch. You can join her on social media—she is most active on Facebook and Instagram. Or subscribe to her newsletter and you'll immediately receive a free read, be able to tag along with her dog-walking adventures, find out what she's reading when she should be working, and other randomness...along with all her writing news, of course! Find the sign-up form on her website (as well as more about her and her books, of course) at brendamargriet.com.

ALSO BY BRENDA MARGRIET

SILVERBERRY SEDUCTION SEASONED
ROMANCE
Secrets Under the Covers
Loving Between the Lines
Turn the Next Page
Strictly by the Book
Too Good for Words
The Complete Silverberry Seduction Series
(e-book only)

TIMELESS SEASONED ROMANCE
After Words
Richly Deserved

THE BENDIXON SISTERS SERIES
Allegro Court
Gateway Crescent
Crossroads Corner
Taking His Measure: The Complete Bendixon Sisters
Series (e-book only)

STANDALONE READS
Mountain Fire
Reserved for You
No Life But This
When Time Falls Still
The Promise of Frost

Read excerpts and find buy links at
www.brendamargriet.com